Duncan Crookes Tovey

Reviews and essays in English literature

Duncan Crookes Tovey

Reviews and essays in English literature

ISBN/EAN: 9783337203337

Printed in Europe, USA, Canada, Australia, Japan

Cover: Foto ©Andreas Hilbeck / pixelio.de

More available books at **www.hansebooks.com**

REVIEWS AND ESSAYS IN
ENGLISH LITERATURE

GEORGE BELL & SONS

LONDON: YORK ST., COVENT GARDEN
NEW YORK: 66, FIFTH AVENUE, AND
BOMBAY: 53, ESPLANADE ROAD
CAMBRIDGE: DEIGHTON, BELL & CO.

REVIEWS AND ESSAYS

IN

ENGLISH LITERATURE

BY

THE REV. DUNCAN C. TOVEY, M.A.

Clark Lecturer at Trinity College, Cambridge; editor of "Gray and his Friends"; "Thomson's Poetical Works," etc.

LONDON
GEORGE BELL AND SONS
1897

CHISWICK PRESS:—CHARLES WHITTINGHAM AND CO.
TOOKS COURT, CHANCERY LANE, LONDON.

To M. T.

MADAM,

In dedicating this volume to you, I presume upon the kindness which has placed at my disposal the sketch (signed with your respected initials) with which it concludes.

That sketch, Madam, is like the solitary Tangerine orange (floating at the top in a little lake of syrup) which the lamented Corney Grain was wont to recommend to the young hostess as a simple but sure note of distinction for the otherwise conventional *trifle.*

The critic, in his paltering fashion, dissects and dissects, destroying the vital principle which he is endeavouring to discover—and then you come, and *presto!* the victims revive, quickened by a breath so kindred that they mistake it for their own.

That through you I am enabled "to adorn my page," great boon as it is, is among the least of those many boons which entitle me to subscribe myself,

Madam,

Your obliged and grateful servant,

D. C. TOVEY.

PREFACE

THOUGH the following papers are reprinted, by kind permission, from the " Guardian," it is right to say that that journal is in no way responsible for the opinions here expressed.

The paper on the Teaching of English Literature is written with considerable exaggeration, not so much of fact as of tone. The writer is himself as guilty as any of those whom he impugns ; and states a problem of which he can only offer a partial and tentative solution. His excuse for vehemence must be, that there is so much clamour upon educational questions at the present day, that, in order to be heard, it is necessary to shout.

Some remarks upon certain characteristics of the eighteenth century, borrowed for the writer's life of Thomson, appear now in their original setting in the Essay on Gay.

CONTENTS

REVIEWS AND ESSAYS IN ENGLISH LITERATURE

THE TEACHING OF ENGLISH LITERATURE

I T would be perhaps too much to say that we have a profound mistrust of the value of examinations in English Literature; but we have a rooted conviction that in any of the forms in which they are conducted by the Universities at present, they are producing a definite mischief. Take for instance the Cambridge Local Examinations. That passionate pursuit of accuracy and precision, that deep-rooted suspicion of anything that savours of vague discursive generalization (so often a cover for ignorance), which as a rule distinguishes the University of Cambridge, is in these examinations brought to bear upon a subject which can only be adequately treated upon lines which give ample scope for these or equally glaring blemishes, and enable those who have no real taste, judgment, or knowledge to indulge in unlimited nonsense. It is possible for example to ask for a comment on the dramatic purpose

B

and meaning of Othello's " Put out the light and then —put out the light !" and the question may produce one or two sensible answers which as a test of literary capacity or promise would be far more convincing than the result of any amount of cram work.   But on the other hand it *has* produced, and that not from a schoolboy, but from an undergraduate, the answer, " Othello says this, dallying with the extinguisher." It is much safer and easier to ask for the meaning and derivation of a word, the evidence for the date of a play, the source from which the plot has been derived, or the point of an allusion. But what is the result of this method ?   That hundreds of boys' schools, hundreds of high schools for girls all over the country in eager competition, anxious to advertise the number of their successes achieved in the Cambridge " Locals " are busy months and months beforehand, getting by heart the notes and introduction to the prescribed play of Shakespeare in the Clarendon Press Series. The *notes* and *introduction*, be it remembered, *not* the text ; that is the last thing thought of.[1] The able editor, Mr. Aldis Wright, who has perhaps done more than any living man to make the careful study of Shakespeare possible and the meaning of Shakespeare clear in this portable and inexpensive form to a large number of his countrymen, must find the sweets of success alloyed

[1] There is abundant circumstantial evidence against the young lady who is accused of having fastened down the text with a piece of elastic because it interfered with her reading the notes.

A candidate has been found to affirm that the *notes* to a particular play were written *before* the text.

with some bitterness if he knows that in the minds of the rising generation he has absolutely ousted the great genius whom he has illustrated so well. It is the firm conviction of many schoolboys that Euclid is the work of Euclid's best-known editor; and if it is not proved already to their satisfaction that Shake-speare is the work of Mr. Aldis Wright it will "go nigh to be thought so shortly," and will be a matter of critical and absolutely demonstrable certainty even to some adults in generations yet unborn. Of the reams of paper at this moment in the world and replenished from year to year, inscribed with a perfectly faithful reproduction of Mr. Aldis Wright's notes, it is highly improbable that nothing will survive the wreck of ages. And if one such document so survives it will by many be held to establish beyond question or cavil that Mr. Aldis Wright wrote Shakespeare.[1] There are intelligent persons now who assign that exploit to Bacon on the extremely slender evidence afforded by

---

[1] This was written in 1886. For Dr. Aldis Wright's editions, those of Mr. Verity, which contain more æsthetic criticism, are now from time to time prescribed for these examinations. It is worse to cram opinions than to cram explanatory details. One and the same play is set for junior and senior students, the only difference being that the paper set for the seniors is supposed to be the harder. It is not thus that graduation should be attempted. All that can be expected of young minds—whether they be called senior or junior—is that they should be able to construe their Shakespeare, tell the story of the play, and describe in their own language the characters of the *dramatis personæ*. But a *senior* student might be expected to read more than one play in the year.

his " Promus," evidence which is but dust in the balance compared with the irresistible inferences which will be drawn from a paper which may contain absolutely nothing of Shakespeare, and yet will explain some of the most difficult passages which have been attributed to his hand.

But, it may be asked, must not the candidate at any rate read the text in order to understand the plot? By no means always. Let us suppose, for example, that " As You Like It " is set as the play for examination. The story in Lodge's novel is substantially the same as the plot of the play, and this story is given at all necessary length in the introduction. But most of the characters bear different names, and hence when any details of the plot of " As You Like It " are asked for, half of the several thousand examinees, instead of Orlando write *Rosader*, instead of Oliver *Saladyne*, the usurping Duke appears in their papers as *Torismond*, the banished Duke as *Gerismond*. And the probability is that this is regarded as quite a trifling error for which some examiners might deduct a mark or two and others none at all. It would indeed require an act of courage beyond the reach of any single man to do the absolutely right thing upon this unmistakable evidence of " the cloven hoof," and condemn the whole mass of worse than useless rubbish without further notice to the flames. The shriek of horror and protestation which would rise up from half the middle-class schools in the kingdom at this wholesale destruction of "the labour of the long year" would be overwhelming and irresistible, nor in fact would the University be justified in punishing so severely the educational blunders which its methods had encouraged.

The only way to lead young minds to a real knowledge of Shakespeare is to induce them to love him. This is a much more difficult task than is commonly supposed, and even Charles and Mary Lamb have achieved but a partial success in attempting it. Its difficulty has increased since their day, because counter-attractions have enormously multiplied. Even with no such temptations in the way, to appreciate Shakespeare when he is easiest requires in most cases the experience of life; to interpret him when he is hardest taxes the resources even of practised and subtle understandings. Yet the spirit of Shakespeare can be caught by many adults and *some* young people simply by *reading* Shakespeare; and, this first step achieved, the exacter study of his text becomes a labour of love. We know an excellent man of business who has much of Shakespeare by heart, and whose comments upon his genius and his characters, if less ambitious than those of some erudite Germans, are at least as sensible, who makes use of various annotators and of Schmidt's "Shakespeare Lexicon" in a way which would gratify the heart of the most rigid of examiners.

The study of English Literature in middle-class schools might be expected ultimately to exercise a refining influence—or, at any rate, to expurgate some of the forms of speech which are transforming, but by no means beautifying the English language. How far the methods by which this study is promoted are on the way to produce this result in the long run may be guessed by the fact that a goodly proportion of the candidates who are examined in the " Merchant of Venice " will tell us that " the leaden casket contains Portia's *photo*."—and one of them has been known to state on the strength of the song which has been cleverly adapted as a baker's advertisement, that Shakespeare uses " fancy " in the sense of " fancy bread." The boy imbued with letters (save the mark!) on such a system sometimes developes into the undergraduate, who in his Little-go—we cite a fact—writes his translation from the Greek of the New Testament, "He did not many wonderful works there *on a/c* of their unbelief." These instances may be straws, but they are straws which show which way the wind is blowing. Demos is well represented now at Cambridge, no less than in the local centres to which Cambridge extends her influence, and so is that other king named Dinos, the mechanical principle, who has expelled Zeus. When Dinos cross-questions Demos he leaves vulgarity unchecked; and the disgusted Spirit of Literature, always something of a truant, and only with the greatest tact and management to be beguiled into a formal examination, goes off elsewhere.

The truth is that the philologers are masters of this field. This is the danger of *all* examinations in literature; it is the inevitable result of such examinations when conducted on a large scale. It is impossible to estimate the relative merits of several thousand boys and girls if a subject is proposed as a test of their taste, or their incipient love of letters ; it is easy enough to do so, if it is proposed as a test of their memories and their knowledge of the meaning of words or phrases. But let us cherish no illusions. We have as little chance of recommending literature to the youthful mind by these disintegrating processes as the simpleton in the old Greek story had of selling his house by carrying about a brick of it as a sample.

Again, we have the highest respect for Grimm's Law, yet we cannot at times repress a sigh for the good old days before this terrible instrument of torture was placed in the teacher's or examiner's hand. Armed with the mighty mace of giant *Grimm*, the modern philologer is abroad in the land like a new iconoclast, smashing to pieces all the most precious monuments of literature. The time may have gone by when a lecturer on Wordsworth could devote two or more lectures to the analysis of the poet's name by means of this formidable implement. But there still exists, we believe, an edition for the use of schools of the " Lay of the Last Minstrel," which is prefaced by a faithful statement of the " Law." There, at any rate, if we may adapt Milton,

" That *tremendous* engine at the door
Stands ready to smite once, and smite no more."

Down before it goes Sir Walter with all his chivalry,

and minstrel and moss-trooper are pounded to a mummy for the imagination of the schoolboy for ever. We do not much care to know what was the precise educational aim in this particular case. We are sure that these and kindred efforts can have but one practical result. It is quite possible that some promising young soul, if the modern schoolmaster would but leave him alone, might be caught by the swing and rush of heroic verse, and inspired with a genuine enthusiasm. But his tormentor interferes, and seizes him almost literally by the throat in the middle not only of sentences but of words and syllables, and all the poor boy's poetic life is squeezed out of him as surely and under the same absurd circumstances as the vital spark was extinguished in the vanquished combatant in " The Critic," who would have added "—nity " but was forced to leave the victor to add it for him. We can picture the scene. The boy is reading or reciting from the " Lady of the Lake ":

> " Unwounded from the dreadful close
> But breathless all Fitz—— "

" Stop, Jones ! what is the meaning and derivation of the prefix *Fitz ?* " And having disposed of Fitz, the tyrant proceeds to demolish James and all the Jacobean dynasty, Jacob (with a plunge into Old and New Testament history), Jacopo, Giacomo, Iachimo, Iago (annexing here all the territory between Venice and Compostella with an expedition across the Atlantic if time permits, and all the range of literature from Shakespeare to the *Acta Sanctorum*), Jaques (with Shakespeare again and a good *casus belli* and plea for invading France in the Jacquerie and Jean Jacques Rousseau), and Yakoob Khan (with a conspectus of contemporary events in Afghanistan, and a general sketch of the history of the British Empire in India).

If there are some who may accuse us of exaggerating here we comfort ourselves with the certain knowledge that there are many long-suffering persons, old and young, who are aware that this is " ower true a tale," and that a teacher who should follow the plan here just faintly indicated would be very generally regarded as a person of some resource who might always be trusted to "make a lesson." The man that does these things should be punished like false Sextus. He should

> " see strange visions
> Which none besides may see,"

even as already, thanks to philology

> " strange sounds are in his ears
> Which none may hear but he."

The pure Spirit of Poetry whom he has outraged should sit beside his bed through the watches of the night and

> " sing of great old houses
> And fights fought long ago,"

and his tongue should cleave to the roof of his mouth in unavailing struggles to interrupt her " sweet voice and low," and bid her derive, and parse, and construe.

She should sing her immortal song this time quite to
the end, and he should be compelled to listen ; she
should sing it

"until the east was grey,
Then, pointing to her bleeding breast,
Should shriek, and flee away."

We have before us an edition of the first book of the
" Excursion " " for the use of schools." In the first
three lines we are pulled up in the notes four times.
Of these four interruptions one is made in order to
derive " landscape," the other to explain "downs "
which we are told mean "high flats. For the meaning
of *flat* compare (passage quoted) Milton's ' Paradise
Lost,' bk. iv., 252 ; for the meaning of *height*, compare
(passage quoted) Gower ' Confessio Am.,' bk. iv."

What man with a brain and a heart would not watch
with interest mixed with anxiety a boy who should be
led by a taste and "natural piety " beyond his years to
read such a poem as the " Excursion "? The gentle
creature should be watched and guarded, but in this
matter he should be dealt with very tenderly. He
should be sent out to play that he might be as like
other boys as possible, in the possession of the health
and elastic spirits and manly fortitude which he is sure
to need more than others in the petty persecution to
which a character so exceptional is likely to be exposed;
but the same kind eye and voice should help him to
remain as unlike them as God meant him to be in the
things of the mind. The fragile little craft should be
carefully steered between the Scylla of morbid and

unsociable priggishness, and the Charybdis of athletic twaddle and small talk which hopelessly engulphs every other topic in the modern schoolboy's imagination. The sanctuary of that soul where a little *cultus* is maintained which is not far from the worship of the Highest should be guarded by discretion and tact, and a policy of non-interference apparent rather than real, with occasional private hints of sympathy and the most marked absence, at any rate, of any official encouragement of that tyrannous inanity which is not only sublimely satisfied with itself, but would reduce everything abnormal in the boy-world in which it reigns supreme to its own dead level. But *Dis aliter visum*. This is but guerilla warfare in the judgment of the modern and omnipotent drill-sergeants of the human mind. To temper the premature love of poetry in the few and to excite it in the many there is but one and the same sovereign method—it is to pack both the few and the many into the same anatomical museum and show them her skeleton. We have as good a right as another, even though that other were a German, to discover the true meaning of Hamlet ; and Hamlet is, in our judgment, the prototype and prophecy of the new pedagogue in

> "inky cloak
> And customary suit of solemn black"—

improving before his youthful audience the dry bones of the dictionary and bidding these dry bones get them to the chamber of my lady Poesy, and tell her " let her paint an inch thick yet to this favour she must come."

We take up next to the book which started these reflections a little volume so like it in shape and size and binding that the one might easily be mistaken for the other. It is a selection of scenes from the " Electra " of Euripides by Mr. Arthur Sidgwick. Mr. Arthur Sidgwick has given a new impulse, a new lease of life to the study of Greek as a necessary element in public school education.   He has headed a revolt against that treatment of the Greek and Latin classics in schools which has made them nothing but a peg on which to hang the lessons of the grammar and the dictionary.[1]   He has not neglected those lessons ; he has put them in a concise and practical form, with a striking absence of those ponderous technicalities which are in some quarters considered to be necessary to intellectual discipline.   This kindly interpreter between great minds and little ones tries to make the scenes of Attic tragedy and comedy alive once more in the schoolroom by giving gestures to the characters and tones to their voices.   The tragic tale, judiciously shortened, can now be read to its climax in one school term instead of being discarded when half told for another, to the utter ruin of all possible interest in the development of the plot.   The effect and, we believe, the intention of all this is at once to excite an interest

[1] The schoolboy who translated

ὃς ᾔδη τά τ' ἐόντα τά τ' ἐσσόμενα πρό τ' ἐόντα,

"who knew both the present and the future and *the future perfect*," is a typical and *suggestive* instance of the occasional results of this method.

in the theme, and to make that interest combine with
sound and sufficient grammatical knowledge as a guide
to the meaning expressed in an extremely difficult
language.   Of all incentives to acquiring an unknown
tongue, strong curiosity is the most potent, and a man
with no linguistic ability has often been known to
master under this impulse a language in which he can
find the best treatment of the subjects in which he is
most keenly interested.   And as no man can be a
perfect scholar who is without the intellectual curiosity
which includes a literary interest in the masterpieces of
the ancient world, so many a mind perhaps incapable
of the highest scholarship may be won to a certain
measure of scholarship by the same attraction.   But
here is the point of this apparent digression.   If Mr.
Sidgwick's method is right, the method of the editor
of Wordsworth's "Excursion" must certainly be wrong.
If in order that the spirit of literature may be seized
it is right to economize the treatment of words and
structure even in an unknown tongue, it must be wrong
to multiply impediments of this kind in a tongue
perfectly familiar.   The difficulty which the young
find in Wordsworth lies not in Wordsworth's language,
but in the immaturity of the youthful mind, and a boy
who in order to understand the "Excursion" really
needs an explanation of such words as "downs"
and "landscape" ought to be studying not the "Excursion," but the horn-book.   But the truth is we are
beginning the reign of pedantry in English just when
we are dropping it in Greek.   And, oddly enough,

these diametrically opposite movements *seem* to be part of the same educational effort, and appear in the same form and from the hands of the same publishers. Messrs. Rivington will, we are sure, excuse us for comparing them to Penelope, who was a most virtuous and industrious person. But we must point out to them that all the educational web which they are weaving in the daylight of Mr. Arthur Sidgwick they are undoing in the dark night of some at least of their editors of the English Classics. And they have not Penelope's excuse ; for their object should be to attract juvenile and, at present, by no means ardent suitors, whilst hers was to repel suitors more mature and importunate. If these two lines of effort which they are encouraging simultaneously meet with the success which both are equally adapted to achieve, we predict a singular result. It will be of paramount importance what subjects we select for study in Greek literature, whilst for English literature this consideration will be of absolutely no importance whatever. As the philological method of interpretation, fostered by teachers and examiners because it is the easiest to manage, prevails more and more, it will gradually dawn upon the schoolmaster that to go to Scott and Wordsworth for the nails by which to fasten the " anatomy " of language is to travel rather far. By the time that he has learnt on the one hand to open the youthful mind to the fascinations of dramatic art in the pages of Euripides and Aristophanes, he will have discovered on the other that he has the raw material of verbal criticism ready to his hand in the songs of the nursery. Common sense and economy will combine to encourage a method of instruction in "English Literature" which, while differing in no essential respect from that which he is at present pursuing, will outrage no sentiments of reverence, will beget no life-long antipathy to letters, and will require no other machinery than a black-board and a piece of chalk ; and he will gently lead his pupils from the study of pathos in the "Alcestis" and of wit and humour in the "Knights" to the exposition of "Ba Ba Black Sheep," by the aid of Grimm's law.

There are few well-trained classical scholars who do not occasionally regret that the habit of minute attention to words and structure begotten by the long discipline through which they have passed mars their power of reading continuously, and consequently of contemplating the total effect of the great works of ancient literature. They may try to forego this habit for a while, to read Homer with no thought of Homer's many commentators, and without turning to the Lexicon for the meaning of a word which they may chance to have forgotten ; but this comparative holiday of the mind hardly to be won over Homer becomes harder still to procure over Æschylus, and quite impossible over Thucydides. The acquired conscience, like the innocent mania of Johnson and De Morgan for touching *all* the railings, keeps teasing till it gets its rights, and the haunting word or note is hunted up after all, just as after a hesitating pause and shuffle on the pavement, the omitted railing is revisited and religiously touched. We are not assailing the system which, if attended by this drawback, has produced so many accurate and subtle minds, but we submit that the intellect is not always to be curbed with bit and bridle, "like horse and mule which have no understanding," and that even horses and mules are sometimes sent out to grass. Modern literature is the playground of the mind which has received its special discipline elsewhere. The difficulties of language which we multiply in Greek and Latin we ought, at any rate, to minimize here. In particular, young and promising scholars should be encouraged to draw from the "fresh woods and pastures new" of English literature which are open to them, without any fence or hedge of linguistic difficulty, the quickening spirit which they may infuse into the dry bones of classical study and make them live again. Much that they have to learn in the schoolroom is only not pedantry, because it is discipline; that they should approach Scott and Wordsworth[1] in the same way is pedantry without excuse. If this sort of thing goes on, if the

[1] There is abundant reason for annotating Milton or Shakespeare, or Spenser or Chaucer. There is ample justification for such an edition as the selections from Burke, with the excellent commentary of Mr. Payne in the Clarendon Press Series, as well as for the edition of Pope's "Essay on Man," and "Satires," by Mr. Mark Pattison. There is, in short, good reason for editing with explanatory notes every book the meaning and spirit of which cannot be seized without them. But such editions as we name are just as necessary for adults as for boys.

rigid educationalist is allowed to say, like a new Æneas, boasting this time of suffering not endured but inflicted by himself—

" Quae regio in terris nostri non plena laboris ? "

the persecuted human spirit will nowhere find asylum, but, as Cicero says to Marcellus, wherever we are, we shall be equally in the power of the conqueror.

We remember with gratitude and affection one eminent scholar, who, by precept and example, illustrated that combination of discipline and play of thought which, perhaps because it is so rare already, we are doing our best to make rarer still. The late W. G. Clark advised a young student, by way of bettering his style of translation, to read Clarendon and Jeremy Taylor, and he was accustomed to preface his lectures to freshmen by suggestive remarks, expressed with the easy grace which distinguished all he said, which just indicated the fact that there was another goal beyond that of verbal criticism. He would link, for example, the ancient and the modern world by points of contrast or comparison, citing an instance of a modern simile from a now forgotten poet, Alexander Smith, who compares the flux and reflux of the sea to a bridegroom, who, admiring his bride—

" Falls back a space to see how fair she be,
Then straight runs up to kiss her,"

and pointing out how foreign is such a fancy to the simpler and severer spirit of ancient poetry.

C

Why should it be so generally assumed as it is in practice that there is no *via media* between dilettantism and pedantry in the treatment of English literature ? There is the historical method, of all methods, in our judgment, the most fruitful and satisfactory. The late Professor J. S. Brewer, in his lectures at King's College, London, almost invariably treated literature in close connection with history, explaining the literature of every epoch by the light of the movements and tendencies of which it was the expression. These lectures were not, we believe, considered to "pay" for the purposes of any examination held outside the walls of the college. But there are many, if we mistake not, who owe that solid and profound scholar a debt of gratitude for habits of thought which are more and better than any temporary success. A good historian with a love of letters—and these two qualifications are in practice inseparable—is an excellent teacher of English literature ; his feet are always on solid ground, and his head is never in the clouds. The spirit of the age as exhibited in the world of action he finds reflected in the world of thought, and he starts at any rate with a clear and distinct mental picture, to the main outlines of which we may always confidently trust. There are no more instructive lessons in the elements of criticism than the chapters on literature in the pages of our great historians ; some of these may be men with limited sympathies, and there may be depths, especially in poetry, which they make no attempt to sound, but as a rule they speak what they see and know, and of things really to be seen and known.

There is a certain contempt now in vogue, especially among schoolmasters, for manuals of English literature. To our thinking these works are among the most satisfactory of the efforts which have been made to impart a knowledge of the subject. There are many books which it is no disgrace not to have read, but which it is discreditable not to know something about. We would rather boys did not read Swift, and we should think little of the wisdom and discretion of any one who put into a boy's hands the " Tale of a Tub." But it is not well that any one should pass as an educated man who does not even know as much about Swift's place in literature as these manuals will tell him. No one is to be blamed for not having read " The Vision of William concerning Piers the Plowman," but the scope and significance of that poem, and the epoch to which it belongs, should be known by everybody. It is as justifiable to get our knowledge about many books at second hand as it is to learn many facts of history without searching the State papers. This concession is made to the limitations of the mind and the brevity of human life in every other study except that of literature. There alone we seem to admit no compromise between the minutest examination of particular authors and a stupendous affectation of original research of the widest compass, sometimes attended with results at once absurd and deplorable.

But, above all, let the schoolmaster encourage play

of mind and do something to keep the mind's play-ground wholesome.   Men despise the old days when the soul was fed on Latin verses, and those days are gone past recall.   Nevertheless the New Zealander who is to discover so many relics of our ruined civilization, whilst he will find very few evidences indeed that the English boy was capable of thought or imagination on his own account in the year 1886, if he lights upon a mouldering copy of the "Musæ Etonenses," may find the indications which he misses for 1886 discoverable in abundance for the period between 1796 and 1833.   This was not because of the Latin verse, which, as the vehicle of thought, is a trick which can be acquired by practice by very unthinking minds.   But the food on which the spirit of the public school boy is nourished has at all times been only very partially supplied in the classroom.   And if at this present epoch he is too often in mind a child, when he ought to begin to be a man, it is because his parents and the public insist at the same time that he shall be a splendid animal, and that his mental powers shall be frittered away upon every branch of knowledge under the sun, with methods necessarily imperfect but often needlessly mechanical.   The first of these conditions he fulfils completely to their satisfaction and his own ; against the second his mind rebels with a reaction either voluntary or involuntary.   The little leisure which is left to him after the one duty has been con-scientiously fulfilled, and the other dealt with at best in a spirit of compromise, he devotes to the records of athletics, the perusal of the society journals, and the reading, often so edifying, which he can enjoy in the daily papers. His novel, if he ever reads a novel, has been described by the typical title "The Blue-nosed Bandit : a Tale of Blood, in three vols., bound in yellow." What power have Scott and Dickens and Thackeray over a mind on which this terrific outlaw exercises his ghoul-like fascinations? An eminent schoolmaster of a past generation thought " Pickwick " and " Punch " were vitiating the taste and checking the reflective powers of the young of his time. Few boys now can appreciate " Pickwick," and we shall not be suspected of exact agreement with all Mr. Punch's judgments when we say that we sincerely wish that our boys were capable of enjoying his wit and humour. The ocean of bad taste which is now deluging them will soon sweep away from their minds the last traces of his amiable reign. It is an ocean which needs a strong breakwater to keep it out, and it is quite beyond the control of any pedagogic Mrs. Partington with her philological mop.

MORE'S UTOPIA [1]

THE problem of More's opinions is in some respects so intricate that it is not surprising that there should be but scant *consensus* on the subject. Yet we confess that we see little or nothing, at least in his " Utopia," that is not explicable as the conclusion, true to the standpoint for the time being assumed, of a comprehensive and severely logical mind. Of his actions indeed, and of his subsequent opinions, a somewhat different account must be given. Here he undoubtedly suffered through the official position which was forced upon his retiring and meditative disposition, through the influence of the monarch whose character he penetrated, and whose despotic authority he had rejected in speculation but often in practice obeyed against the grain, through a contempt for the judgments and convictions of the unlettered (the common error of learning at that time), resulting in a line of conduct towards these which contrasted not only in fact but in spirit with his theoretical advocacy of liberty of thought ; and through the violence of civil and religious reformers, which threw him into a reactionary attitude

[1] "Sir Thomas More." By W. H. Hutton, B.D. Methuen.

and made him a zealous advocate of impugned doctrines
and institutions which had possessed at one time but
little attraction for him. Nor when he answered a
coarse attack upon the religious orders, can he have
forgotten that he had himself in his " Utopia " lent
much countenance to the plainer speech of vulgar men
on the subject. The desire which he himself at one
time entertained for monastic seclusion was quite compatible with the conviction—reasonable or otherwise—
that these institutions had been multiplied to excess,
and fostered much idleness to the detriment of the
State. We are of opinion that the whole of the
" Utopia " is to be taken, with differences indeed of
standpoint, quite seriously. And if any parts of it
have a direct purpose, these, it is admitted, are such as
comment upon European, and particularly English,
institutions. It is More, and only ostensibly Raphael
Hythlodaye, who exclaims (near the beginning of the
second book), " How great and how idle a company is
there of priests and religious men, as they call them,"
unless we are to suppose that More thus wantonly insinuates, without controverting, an opinion which he did
not himself entertain on an important topic of the day.
To the same purport is one of the liveliest passages in
the first book—the conversation in which Hythlodaye
professes to have taken part at Cardinal Morton's table.
There a proposal is made by a certain jesting parasite
or scoffer that all beggars shall be distributed and
bestowed into houses of religion, the men to be made
lay brethren and the women nuns. Whereupon a

certain friar, graduate in divinity—albeit "a man of
grisly and stern gravity," enters into the spirit of the
thing, and insists that some provision shall be made
also for friars. "Why," said the jester, "that is done
already, for my lord himself (the Cardinal) set a very
good order for you when he decreed that vagabonds
should be kept strait and set to work ; for you be the
greatest and veriest vagabonds that be." Upon which
the friar could not refrain himself from chiding, scold-
ing, railing, and reviling ; and in the course of his heat
this graduate in divinity gives samples of his skill in
the application of Scripture, of which this one shall
suffice :

"If many scorners of Helizeus, whiche was but one bald
man, felt the zeal of the bald, how much more shall one
scorner of many friars feel, among whom be many bald
men?" "And we have also," he adds, "the Pope's Bulls,
whereby all that mock and scorn us be excommunicate,
suspended and accursed."

The scene is Erasmus's "Encomium Moriae," in
little ; the method of Erasmus dramatized ; Folly set
to work to anatomize folly, and to bring into view the
indolence and arrogance of these men, the perverse
and barbarous ingenuity of their pretensions to learning, and the abuse of the highest spiritual authority in
championing them. If, as Mr. Hutton tells us (somewhat boldly, as we think), More's views were throughout his life in substantial accordance with those of
Erasmus, this was emphatically the case in the days of
the "Utopia" and "Encomium." It is strange indeed

to note how these fraternal minds went for a time *pari passu*. Perhaps even More's unfinished devotional treatise " Memorare Novissima " was suggested to his mind by Erasmus's " Enchiridion Militis Christiani." Perhaps, on the other hand, a comparison might bring out a characteristic difference between these two kindred spirits. In the " Enchiridion " the man of letters, and even the dialectician, is almost as much in evidence as the Christian moralist. Writing in Latin, Erasmus never forgets the Latinist, and his extreme classicism of language and allusion gives to his book a semblance of unreality which perhaps does not belong to it. The point of contact between the two books is their simplicity on the doctrinal side ; but More's sincerity strikes home because he writes in his native tongue ; in this province, on the other hand, as in his elaborate and pungent satire, Erasmus leaves on us the impression of mental rather than moral force. It is harder to distinguish the two men in intellect than in temperament up to the point at which temperament and circumstances come into play, and investigation would disclose many resemblances indicating their close community in thought and study. One harmony between "Utopia " and the " Colloquies " has especially struck us—the reconciliation of the Epicurean theory of pleasure with religion :

" The Utopians," says More, " reason of virtue and pleasure. . . . In this point they seem almost too much given and inclined to the opinion of them, which defend pleasure, wherein they determine either all or the chiefest part of man's felicity to rest.   And (which is more to be marvelled at) the defence of this so dainty and delicate an opinion they fetch even from their grave, sharp, bitter, and rigorous religion.   For they never dispute of felicity or blessedness, but they join unto the reasons of philosophy certain principles taken out of religion. . . . Those principles be these and such like; that the soul is immortal, and by the bountiful goodness of God ordained to felicity; that to our virtues and good deeds rewards be appointed after this life, and to our evil deeds punishments."

In the last of his "Colloquies" Erasmus makes Hedonius maintain with success that, " Nulli magis sunt Epicurei quam Christiani bene viventes."   This view is familiar enough now, but it was, possibly, More who first gave it definite expression, and the best evidence that it was startling is the pains which Erasmus subsequently took to pretend that the opinion was that of the person of the dialogue, and not his own.   Erasmus is generally, we believe, more successful in attack than in apology ; his defence of the "Colloquies," in this and in other particulars, might be called disingenuous, if it were not transparent.   More, in the very form of his " Utopia," leaves himself everywhere a much safer *locus poenitentiae ;* in the land of Nowhere his mind was at large, whatever restrictions his faith might impose on it ; his delicate but effective irony could there work at will.   What could be more pointed, and at the same time more unassailable, than the simple statement that the Utopians " have priests of exceeding holiness, and, *therefore*, very few ? "   And whilst we have all admired

a thousand times the scene in which Gulliver rouses
the wrath and disgust of the Brobdingnagian, by describing the skill of Europeans in the invention and
use of weapons of destruction, it may be questioned
whether More, less vigorous and less misanthropic
than Swift, is not more adroit and practical in his
picture of the Utopian methods of war. Here let us
quote Mr. Hutton's effective summary, which well explains More's real drift :

"The Utopians abhor war, and fight only in defence of
their own country, or to defend some oppressed nation.
They fight also, by preference, with cunning, to avoid blood-
shed. They offer large bribes for the assassination of the
chiefs of their adversaries, and for treason among their
enemies. Here the inference was obvious. If these actions
seemed a detestable contrast to the lofty morality of the
Utopians, much more was it a dishonour to a Christian
Government to engage in such intrigues as at that very time
Henry VIII. was carrying on in Scotland. An equally severe
condemnation is employed in the Utopians' employment of
mercenaries. It could have needed no acute intelligence to
recognize the Swiss—whom the King was then employing
—in the Zapoletes, 'dwelling in wild woods and high
mountains,' who basely hire themselves to the highest bidder,
and whom it would be well if war had utterly destroyed."

In no way could More have better exhibited his
intense horror of war than in his picture of it as
practised by a peace-loving but severely logical people.
Still more scathing, as a censure upon European
politics, and yet, as Mr. Hutton remarks, without any-

thing which authority could reprehend, is the beautiful
irony with which the Utopians are represented as—

" Making no leagues, chiefly because that in those parts of
the world leagues between princes be wont to be kept and
observed very slenderly. *For here in Europe, and especially
in those parts where the faith and religion of Christ reigneth,
the majority of leagues is everywhere considered holy and in-
violable; partly through the justice and goodness of princes,
and partly at the reverence and motion of the head Bishops.*
Which, like as they make not promises themselves but they
do very religiously perform the same, so they exhort all
princes in any wise to abide by their promise, and them
that refuse or deny so to do, by their Pontifical power and
authority they compel thereto.   And surely they think well
that it might seem a very reproachful thing if, in the leagues of
them which by a peculiar name be called faithful, faith should
have no place.   But in that new-found part of the world "—

things, he goes on to say, are very different.   There
kings and princes practise a crafty dealing which those
who advise them to it would be the loudest to condemn in private men ; as if justice was something far
under the dignity of kings ; or as if there were two
justices, one meant for the inferior sort of people, the
other a princely virtue of more majesty and liberty
"to which nothing is unlawful that it lusteth after."
" There could be no clearer reprobation," says Mr.
Hutton, " of any difference between political and
individual morality."

We know of no reason for believing that More ever
altered his opinions on questions of political justice or
of social life ; due regard being had to his function as

administrator of the laws as they then stood. But when Mr. Hutton, in commenting on the " Dialogue," of which the first edition appeared in 1529, tells us that " There is no reason to assume that More's views had changed since he wrote the ' Utopia,' and the distinct declaration of them in his controversial works seems to prove that no importance is to be attached to the ideal picture of religion in the happy island " he seems to us to say too much. It is surely paradoxical to suppose that a deeply religious man, writing under one and the same disguise, meant much when he treated of morals and justice, and nothing at all when he treated of religion. We quite understand Mr. Hutton to mean that More's own doctrinal opinions were always fixed. Yet, however this may be, Mr. Hutton's statement certainly obscures the fact that More's theory of toleration quite fell to pieces. If he could maintain, after his resignation of the Chancellorship, that heresy, being a great crime against God, deserved a severe punishment from the secular power, he certainly departed from the suggestive wisdom of King Utopus. When More writes of him : "*Though there be one religion which alone is true*, and all other vain and superstitious, *yet did he well foresee* (so that the matter were handled with reason and sober modesty) that the truth of the[1] (*its*) own power would, at the last issue, out and come to light ": he is surely not only stating but commending that

---

[1] The version of Robynson, who does not know "*its.*"

opinion, and urging it indirectly, as the right policy for the one true Church. It is scarcely necessary to remark that this is in the very spirit of Erasmus, and with that spirit More certainly ceased, both in practice and in theory, to be " in substantial accordance " on this important topic. The excesses of all kinds which he traced to the progress of the religious revolution led him to reconsider the whole question, and to abandon what was once a first principle to him. Having to execute measures of repression, he was glad to persuade himself that these were in accordance with his conscience, as well as with his official duty. We have seen it stated that " Utopia " was motived by More's desire to make his convictions quite clear to his royal master before becoming bound to his service. This, if it be so, gives a serious colour to every speculation in the work which has a bearing upon a present state of things, and prevents us from accepting Hallam's suggestion that the book is one of those which men of genius throw off in gaiety of heart, though we may readily admit that it was written without much suspicion of the new power of literature to set ideas fermenting in the world at large. The sixteenth century offers in this respect a striking parallel to the eighteenth. Both More and Montesquieu sat in their studies and satirized and speculated without suspecting that they were sowing a crop for Smithfield or the guillotine. For this pardonable blindness More paid a severer penalty than Erasmus, his colleague in emancipating the mind ; both were aghast at the extravagances to which the freedom of thought which they advocated had given birth ; but only More had to visit these with imprisonment and death.

We believe that More's strongest revolt was against schism rather than heresy. Mr. Hutton, if we do not mistake, would make his primary conviction from first to last the idea of the unity of Christendom, the Universal Church. When he clearly saw that this was menaced, he took alarm and abandoned the hope which he had once cherished with Erasmus of a Church which should admit great variety of opinion without rupture. The Utopians are represented as Monotheists of various sorts, among whom Christianity has only begun to spread. But we cannot believe that because they are not Christians the picture of the unity in worship which they achieved was without significance or suggestion. It was obvious and safe so to describe them that censure or admonition might fall only indirectly upon Christian authorities, and the moral might be admitted or disclaimed according to circumstances. But we select one instance, out of several, in which " they which do not agree to Christ's religion " must certainly be supposed to read a lesson to those who do :

"One of our company in my presence was sharply punished. He, as soon as he was baptized, began against our wills, with more earnest affection than wisdom to reason of Christ's religion, and began to wax so hot in his matter, that he did not only prefer our religion before all other, but also did utterly despise and condemn all others, calling them profane, and the followers of them wicked and devilish and the children of everlasting damnation. When he had thus long reasoned the matter, they laid hold on him, accused him, and condemned him into exile, not as a despiser of religion, but as a seditious person and a raiser up of dissension among the people."

The only forces which the Utopians permitted in the propagation of religion were argument or persuasion, and prayer; they immediately and severely repressed not only violent methods, but violent language in a religious cause. A signal instance of this is a Catholic using in Utopia the language common in Europe about heretics, and promptly punished in consequence. Here the drift is quite unmistakable. And so also, we believe, is the drift of those passages which describe the common worship of their various sects. They point to that unity in diversity which More then believed to be possible in the Catholic Church.

These side glances at the religious life of Christendom, as More knew it, are not altogether reproachful. The dim light which the Utopians preferred in their churches, "because they thought that overmuch light doth disperse men's cogitations," More himself knew and loved; with "the unhurtful and harmless kind of worship" in "frankincense and a great number of wax candles and tapers" which pleased them, he himself was pleased. Mr. Hutton is undoubtedly right in maintaining that their sacerdotal vestments and the

homage paid to the priests as they enter the church
have a significance like that of the Catholic ritual.
The point of difference is only evidence of More's
minute attention to consistency. He has described
the Utopians as despising and abhorring gold, and
making it a badge of infamy, and gems and precious
stones but toys and trifles for children. It was therefore necessary that he should describe their priests as
clad in colours excellent in workmanship rather than
materials, and precious because of the pains and skill
which devotion had expended upon them; and, besides, More thus has an opportunity of hinting how
much more real an offering such labour is than the
easy and indolent profusion with which wealthy men
in Europe brought their gifts to the altar. And we
agree with Mr. Hutton that no inference as to More's
view on the place of images and pictures in Catholic
worship can be drawn from the bare statement that
the Utopians " have no image of any god in the church,
to the intent it may be free for every man to conceive God by their religion after what likeness and
similitude they will." It should, indeed, be obvious
that this is a necessary corollary to the statement
that the church was the meeting-place for common
worship between sects whose symbolism, when they
worshipped apart, varied with no limitation whatever.
In fact, thus much More expressly states: "The
common sacrifices," he says, "be so ordered that they
be no derogation nor prejudice to any of the private
sacrifices and religions." Further, we agree with Mr.

D

Hutton that the opinion of the Utopians makes nothing against celibacy as the rule of the Roman priesthood, or against fasting as practised by the faithful and by More himself. Nay, it seems to us that More's language points the other way. Of the "religious" in Utopia, one sect is single, the other married. The Utopians, says More, count the married the wiser, but the other the holier :

"Which in that they prefer single life before matrimony, and that sharp life before an easier life, if herein they grounded upon reason they would mock them. But now forasmuch as they say they be led to it by religion, they honour and worship them."

In other words, the Utopians were guided in the main by the wisdom and reason of nature ; but they had the candour to acknowledge that there might be a mode of life dictated by a higher inspiration. As we have seen, in view of a future state of blessedness to be attained by it, there was no inconsistency between the practice of this "grave, sharp, bitter, and rigorous religion" and the favourite philosophy of Utopia. We believe, indeed, that More really entertained, with Erasmus, this seeming paradox, and that his gently expressed wonderment is only an ironical disguise. The whole passage in which the life of these rigid ascetics is sketched proves that More would have been patient enough of the ignorance of the Monks, but that he believed them to be lazy. His Utopian celibates, who care nothing for learning, nor "give their mind to any knowledge of things, utterly forsake

and eschew idleness," and undertake all the unpleasant
and hard and vile work which other men refuse. And
More's real sympathy with the principle of monas-
ticism could scarcely be more effectively shown than
in the words describing the conversion of the Utopians
to the Christian faith :

"I think this was no small help and furtherance in the
matter that they heard us say that Christ, instituted, among
His, all things common, and that the same community doth
yet remain *among the rightest Christian companies.*"

There is nothing, we believe, in the whole of the
"Utopia" that is not explicable, either as indirect
comment or counsel, or as a picture of the best conclusions of unassisted human reason. If the Utopians
are allowed under the extremest circumstances, and
then only by the advice and with the sanction of the
priests and magistrates, to seek a voluntary death,
this is surely because More himself had determined
that the wisdom of nature pointed no other way ; and
he limits the practice to cases to which the Socratic
figure of the soldier deserting his post does not apply,
—to sufferers not able to do any duty of life, who, by
"overliving" their own deaths, are noisome and irk-
some to others and grievous to themselves. It is,
however, here, if anywhere, that More's expressed dis-
approval at the end of the work of some of the
Utopian institutions must apply, although he shows
pretty clearly that he means us to draw no inferences
from that general disclaimer, for to the particular in-

stance at which he professes to stumble, the community of goods and the prohibition of money, this
notorious contemner of pomp and splendour both in
office and in private life objects, with fine irony, that
thus "all nobility, magnificence, worship, honour, and
majesty, the true ornaments and honours, as the common opinion is, of a commonwealth, utterly be over-
thrown and destroyed."

The "Utopia" is best understood by admitting
that More had a gift, possessed only by the greatest of
religious minds, the Pascals and Newmans of the
world, the power to follow with a measure of sympathy
the workings of the intellect in the natural man.
It is the most beautiful flower and fruit of the new
humanism planted in the safe soil of the Catholic
faith. The liberal culture by which More so abundantly
profited enabled him to abstract himself from his
beliefs, and to convey lessons, otherwise difficult and
dangerous to deliver, through the picture of a wise
and understanding people, with no guide but the
dictates of right reason, with a theistic creed accepted
as the conclusion of that reason and as a satisfaction
of their emotional needs, and a persuasion no less
reasonable that the Being Whom they worshipped
heard and answered prayer, and could and did make
revelations of His will which had a greater claim to
the obedience of individual souls than the wisdom
which sufficed for the ordinary guidance of life. We
are convinced that, whatever details, of the least importance, More embroidered on this framework repre-

sent his own convictions both as a thinker and a Catholic, and that we can discover there in harmonious fusion the nominalist,[1] the utilitarian, the socialist, and the devout and orthodox Christian. If the book is not a prophecy of the future, it is at least a prophecy of opinion. Nor was there aught, save one thing, in all his subsequent life which can be said, upon a complete view, and with due regard to the functions he was called upon to discharge, to be at variance with the beautiful dream which has made him immortal in the world of thought. If he punished Protestants only for the violence of their language, he acted in accordance with the practice of the Utopians, except that his action here was perforce one-sided, and therefore, though from causes beyond his own control, unjust. But we think we could prove, if we had space, that his zeal against heresy pushed him to greater activity even than his office required.

It is part of his character that if he was once assured that such active zeal was a duty, he would violate his own gentle and humane nature to display it. The man who, as Mr. Hutton finely says, "laid down his life rather than surrender what he again and again admitted to be but an opinion," to whom "almost alone among his contemporaries the conclusions of the intellect seemed no less sacred than the chastity of the body," and who "died rather than tarnish the whiteness of his soul," was little likely to shrink from

[1] "Utopia," p. 107, ed. Lumby. Camb. Univ. Press.

obloquy when called upon to act from conviction. Yet
so essentially benign was his spirit, so sad his destiny
when once entangled in the policies of an evil time,
that every adverse sentiment about him is lost in love,
regret, and pity.   An irony less gentle than that with
which he has played for generations about the hearts
of men forced this soul, all conscience and duty, spite
of shrinkings and forebodings, into the toils of the
moral monster whose opinions shifted with his passions,
and who first taught his victim the doctrine which he
beheaded him for believing. And Rome has done
well to proclaim More a saint, though canonization
is sometimes but the poor and tardy amends which
Churches make when they have inflicted upon otherwise blameless lives the only stains which posterity is
able to discover.

FULLER'S SERMONS [1]

O F all our many English writers whom it is customary to designate as quaint, perhaps Fuller exhibits a quaintness which savours least of antiquity, of affectations now quite obsolete. The invariable note of that Euphuism, of which so many of our prose writers, until the formation of a classic style, had some trace, was an excess of illustration, not natural and spontaneous, but far-fetched and studiously ingenious. Lyly, its prototype, exhausts the animal and vegetable kingdom to enhance a truism. Burton accumulates epithets and multiplies quotations, until it is these, and not his theme, that engage the amused and bewildered mind. Sir Thomas Browne is never happy unless he can express a thought, in itself simple, in the form of an enigma. But Fuller's wit and fancy have their *race*, the flavour of the soil from which they spring ; they belong essentially to a character, uncommon in all ages, yet not limited to any age ; to a combination of quick imagination with a sympathetic temper, hitting upon resemblances too

[1] "The Collected Sermons of Thomas Fuller." J. E. Bailey and W. E. A. Axon, Gresham Press.

remote for ordinary observation, yet not too abstruse to be understood and enjoyed at once. Hence a quaintness such as Fuller's is a recurrent, not an extinct, phenomenon. A clever matron of to-day, when "flitting," found a temporary refuge, with her family, under the hospitable roof of a neighbour, and said to him on entering, "I am afraid you will say, 'Gad, a troop cometh.'" We have found this witticism twice anticipated by Fuller in the volumes before us.

In South, as in Fuller, we have that happy medium of wit, which is the true salt of it, as preserving it from corruption. But South's wit is often marred by its asperity, and never more than faintly coloured by imagination. On the other hand, as Lamb finely says, "Fuller's conceits are oftentimes deeply steeped in human feeling and passion ; " and we recognize almost instinctively that he who called negroes " the Image of God cut in ebony," must have had much of the milk of human kindness. These phrases are a revelation of the inner man, and in the hand of such as Fuller the pen is as expressive as the facial muscles. His loftier fancies, in like manner, deserve to live, because they are really poetic, they have something emotional in them ; our first impulse on reading them is to say, not "How ingenious!" but "How beautiful!" And thus Lamb refuses to call the often-quoted passage about the ashes of Wiclif "a conceit"; he truly pronounces it "a grand conception." As a master of style, Fuller seems to combine with characteristic moderation various attributes—*parti-*

culam undique decerptam—of which his great contemporaries afford more exaggerated examples. He
has something of Milton's vigour in controversy; if
his manner falls short of Milton's Demosthenic force, it
lacks also his un-English structure, his gloom, and
his acerbity; and when Fuller is most uncom-
promising there is in him that touch of humour which,
at least in conversation, is even now held to excuse a
pungent repartee. His "Truth Maintained" is a
temperate document; yet, being arraigned for the
judicious statement that "a Church and a Reformation
will be imperfect, do the best you can," he cannot
help retorting "I said it, and I say it againe; it was a
Truth before your Cradle was made, and will be one
after your Coffin is rotten." This is a trifle brutal;
but we feel that it has been prompted not by animosity,
but by the temptation of a telling antithesis. Milton's
moods are few and always severe; like other great
men, he sinks terribly low, as if in proportion to his
gravity, when in an effort to be popular he sinks at
all. With Fuller the style is always the man; a man
of many moods, yet none of them ill-natured. And so
the expansive picture-writing of Jeremy Taylor is
almost within the compass of his art, as when he
says:

"As Hills, the higher, the barrener; so men, commonly
the wealthier, the worse; the more Honour, the less Holi-
nesse. And as Rivers, when content with a small Channel,
runne sweet and cleare; when swelling to a Navigable
Channel, by the confluence of severall Tributarie Rivulets,

gather mudde and mire, and grow salt and brackish, and violently beare downe all before them ; so many men, who in meane Estates have been Pious and Religious, being advanced in Honour and enlarged in Wealth, have growne bothe impious and prophane towards God, cruell and tyrannical over their brethren."

If he has not Barrow's exhaustiveness, he has a far more vivid imagination, and with something of Barrow's copiousness of language, he marshals his forces better.   As in this :

"Let us all provide for that perfect Reformation in the world to come ; when Christ shall present the Church his Spouse to God his Father, *Without spot,* coming from man's corruption, *or wrincle,* caused by times continuance, When we shall have a *new Heaven and a new Earth, wherein shall dwell Righteousnesse :* With judgements reformed from error, wills reformed from wilfulnesse, affections reformed from mistaking their object, or exceeding their measure ; all powers and parts of soule and body reformed from sin to sanctity."

In these and a thousand passages we find, at some point or other, Fuller's invariable mark of distinction, the charm of antithesis. Lamb, whom nothing escapes, has noted with what admirable address Fuller has employed this perpetual balance in his account of Henry de Essex, where it beguiles us into compassion for a fate which never,' perhaps, engaged much sympathy before, the fate of a coward.   Yet, with all the effect of art, the contrasts which he delights to make are not artificial ; they are in nature, in human life, as he viewed it, and in himself ; and the form in which he presents them is the result not only of a quick apprehension and facile ingenuity, but of large sympathies aided by the clear vision of a world in which the colours of good and evil are inseparably mingled.

We might almost surmise that Fuller's best fancies owe as much to his character as to his intellect, from the fact that he sometimes repeats them ; for we soon tire of thoughts which are so little natural to us, that we have to cudgel our brains to get at them ; and the merely artificial creatures of the mind are never our companions. . If Fuller more than once employs the thought "Conscience is the Attorney-General of the King of Heaven in our Hearts, to press the evidence after the Indictment," it is because this seems to him, once for all, to be the best expression of a felt truth, and he will not go beyond it in search of a novelty more ingenious but less exact. And when Waller writes :

"The soul's dark cottage, batter'd and decayed,
Lets in new light through chinks which time has made,
Stronger by weakness, wiser, men become
As they draw near to their eternal home,"—

we are surprised to find in him of all men a conceit thus steeped in human and religious feeling. Lamb has noted the resemblance to Fuller's words about St. Monica ; but the truth is this is a favourite child of Fuller's genius, born as early as 1633. In a sermon then preached at Cambridge, and repeated often elsewhere, he says of the righteous :

"Grace by custome is made another nature unto them, especially toward the latter end of their lives : partly because their soules do steale a Glymps, Glance, or Pisgah-sight of heaven through the Clefts and Chinkes of their Age- or sick-nesse-broken bodies ; and partly because, as all motion is swiftest the neerest it comes to the Center, so they, the neerer they draw by death to heaven, God's Spirit and all goodnesse groweth more quick and active in them."

The temptation to find a plagiarism where there is no more than a parallel, is often misleading, yet it is perfectly possible that Waller either heard or read these words, in an age when worldlings often listened to sermons, and the horizon of the pulpit was wider than it is now.   On the other hand, when Fuller says in the same discourse " It is the greatest misery that one has once been happy," the resemblance to Dante is probably due to no other cause than the same impression made at different epochs upon a thoughtful mind by the vicissitudes of a troubled world.

" All truths," says Fuller, " have Eagle's eyes," and if his thoughts can face without flinching the sunlight of long experience, it is because they have in them the strength of vision which belongs to perennial truth. His deepest prejudices were perhaps anti-Papal ; yet this does not prevent him, when it was dangerous to say so, from maintaining that no just offence is to be given to the Papists ; or from defending this opinion in a passage which is nothing less than statesmanlike:

" Know, Sir," he writes, "that besides those Papists in *England* and *Ireland* to whom you say the Parliament hath proclaimed an irreconcileable war, there be also many of their Religion in Spaine, France, Germany, Italy, Poland, &c., all *Europe* over, with whom the Parliament hath not as yet professed open hostility, and to these no offence must be given. The eye of all Christendom is upon us; the Sea surrounds, but doth not conceale us. Present Papists read the text of our actions, and their posterity will write comments upon them : we cannot, therefore, be too wary."

Again, in the interpretation of many parts of Old Testament history we in these days are often encumbered with the help that modern criticism offers towards the solution of a moral doubt, and have to confess ourselves disgusted with the transparent artifice which tries to smother up a difficulty in a phrase. When Milman explains the incident of " the enemies of Elijah struck by fifties with lightning," by saying, " The prophets had been infected by the ferocity of the times ; " the merest child can see that he is absolutely incoherent ; and that to those who accept, as he does, the narrative as true, the suggestion that its central fact was altogether due to the working of human passions, must be absurdly false. Far more sane, consistent, and reverent, while not less true to that better spirit of which Christians are, is Fuller's comment, which has at least the permanence which belongs to a faith at unity with itself :

" Elijah, who cursed the Captaines with their fifties, could cause fire to come down on them from Heaven. It appears that his curse was pronounced without malice, because inflicted by a miracle. It is lawfull for such to call for fire,

who can make fire come at their call; and would none
would kindle discord on Earth, till they first fetcht the
sparks thereof from Heaven."

And, whilst we are not now concerned with Fuller's
doctrinal tenets, it is worth while to notice that his in-
clination is to survey controversy in its length and
breadth, and historic consequences in something of
the humane and judicial spirit of Hooker, and therefore its less sinister aspects do not escape him. He
reminds us, as Newman has reminded us, that heresies
may turn to profit in " clearing of truth " :

" Her old Evidences which have been long neglected will
then be searched and found out; her rusty Arguments will
be scoured over and furbished up. Many will run to and
fro, and knowledge shall be increased. Those which before
shooting at the Truth, were over, under, or wide, will now,
with the left-handed Gibeonites, hit the mark at a haires
breadth, and faile not : Many parts of true Doctrine have
bin slenderly guarded, till once they were assaulted by
Heretikes : and many good Authors in those points which
were never opposed, have written but loosely, and suffered
unwary passages to fall from their posting pens. But when
theeves are about the countrey, every one will ride with his
sword and stand on his guard : when Heretikes are abroad
in the world, Writers weigh each word, ponder each phrase,
that they may give the enemies no advantage."

Even when he would be most severe he seems to
divert the shaft when he intends to point it, by some
gentle touch which turns the eye elsewhere, as when
he says : " As children used to say, they love Father

and Mother both best : so let us hate Heresies and
Schisms both worst." And when Mr. John Saltmarsh
Pastor of Hesterton, Yorkshire, attacking Fuller's
Sermon of Reformation, affirms, in that queer Puritan
phraseology, which was often so curiously infelicitous,
that "We may have Beames and Radiations .and
Shootings which our Fathers had not," it is with a
kind of whimsical sadness that Fuller seizes upon an
opening which would be obvious even to a man of less
ready wit in 1643 :

"For *Beames* and *Radiation* of knowledge," he says, "I
have delivered my oppinion ; but as for *Shootings*, God
knows we have many, such as our Fathers never had. God
in his mercy cease such *Shootings*, or else in his Justice
direct the Bulletts to such markes as in truth have been the
troublers of our Israel."

A temper so remote from fanaticism, an understanding so clear as his, was unable to lose, in
enthusiasm for a cause, the sense of the horrors with
which its struggles were accompanied. Surveying the
whole arena with impartial eyes he cannot see the
generic differences between the combatants which we,
who judge from typical examples, are accustomed to
find ; he does not even see, with Chillingworth, "publicans
and sinners on the one side and scribes and Pharisees
on the other." In his "Fast Sermon on Innocents'
Day," preached at the Savoy in 1642, he was on very
treacherous ground ; his audience may have been for
the most part in sympathy with him ; but his undis-
guised loyalty and conspicuous powers must have

made him already an object of suspicion to the authorities then dominant in the capital. Nevertheless it is the boast of superior godliness on the Parliamentarian side that he is deprecating, and he seems to be addressing Roundheads rather than Royalists, when he says :

"The general hindrance (to Peace) is this :—The many national sinnes of our kingdome being not repented of. I say of our kingdome, not of one Army alone. Thinke not that the King's Army is like *Sodome*, not ten righteous men in it (no, not if righteous *Lot* himselfe be put into the number) ; and the other Army like Zion consisting all of Saints. No : there be drunkards on both sides, and swearers on both sides, and whoremongers on both sides ; pious on both sides, and prophane on both sides ; like Jeremies figges, those that are good are very good, and those that are bad are very bad in both parties. I never knew nor heard of an Army all of Saints, *save the holy army of Martyrs;* and those, you know, were dead first; for the last breath they sent forth proclaimed them to be Martyrs."

The novelist and even the historian have found an easier theme in the strong contrasts between the Wildrakes and the Sergeants Bind-their-Kings-in-Chains, between Laud and Hugh Peters, than in the many lights and shades which belong to every great national struggle, as to the most trivial scene of human life. Whether we condemn or praise the Fullers and the Falklands in days of storm and stress, it is from these, the men whose proper province is thought rather than action, the Hamlets of a world out of joint, who look about them with doubt and misgiving amid the tragic scenes in which they are compelled to take a part, without the stern joy of the warrior or the fiery zeal of the partisan to blind them, from these that we must learn that the strife of passions or principles on the large scale is like the encounter of two mighty floods, each of which bears along with it to the final collision a mingled mass of things precious and things vile. It is good sometimes for those who would know the whole truth to converse with the divisions of Reuben in which there are great search-ings of heart, and even with Asher whilst he abides in his breaches. At the battle of Edgehill, Harvey, the discoverer of the circulation of the blood, sits under a hedge with the two young princes in his charge, and reads a book, until an impertinent "bullet of a great gun" disturbs him. The picture may serve as a type of the gentler influences and humanities in evil days working still amid the whirlwind and the fire which menace but cannot destroy them. It is at once rest-ful and helpful to turn the mild light of literature upon history, and thus to discover beautiful and unexpected amenities in fierce times, and a culture or a piety which acknowledged kindred spirits irrespective of faction. Let us modify, for instance, the severe and contemptuous judgment of Clarendon upon Sir John Danvers, the regicide, by the pages before us, which remind us that he was an indulgent stepfather to George Herbert, and, even in the crisis which has tarnished his name, the friend and protector of Thomas

Fuller. He was one of the only two civilians in that strange assize whom the King recognized as known to him before the troubles, indeed " he had been gentleman of the Privy Chamber to Charles, when Prince of Wales "; and his part should have been as unwelcome to him as it was certainly ungracious. The strange companionship between him and Fuller is perhaps none the less pleasant to contemplate, because it is perplexing. His needs and his ambitions may have confused his motives, and yet left him a genuine sympathy with a man whom the times might sadden, but could not corrupt or beguile. We have linked once already Fuller's name with Falkland's; and we cannot better close the remarks suggested by these volumes than with some words of Fuller in which the sad, despondent accents of Falkland's last days seem to be anticipated :

" If I should chance to be stricken dumbe, I would with Zacharia make signes for table bookes and write that the name of that which I desire above all earthly things is Peace."

LETTERS OF THE
EARL OF CHESTERFIELD[1]

CHESTERFIELD is now known chiefly as an educator of youth ; and in that character he does not shine. So different is his moral standpoint from our own, that we can scarcely conceive a state of society in which such precepts could have been read by any class of people without some sense of repulsion. Nor, although Lord Carnarvon is of a different opinion, were we able to discover in the later letters addressed to the godson any indications of a change of tone. If his suggestions then were never quite so profligate, it must be remembered that his second pupil was only a child ; the presence of the old leaven is for all that unmistakable. We are convinced that there was no reformation. The old man had begun to weave a new web for the godson seven years before the son received his last admonitions ; and it would be an easy, but rather painful task, to prove in detail that the fabric of the garment, by no means a garment of righteousness,

[1] "Chesterfield's Letters." Edited by Dr. Bradshaw. (Sonnenschein.)

which he provided for both his disciples, was of the
same material. How, indeed, could it be otherwise?
Out of the abundance of the heart the mouth speaketh;
and Chesterfield's heart, naturally generous, was in
some respects vitiated by the tolerance of his age for
immorality in high places, and by a theory of life
hard, narrow, and cynical. " To talk of natural affection is talking nonsense," he says. He remarks that
a parent and child who had never met before would
not recognize one another at their first meeting, and
he considered this a conclusive proof of his general
thesis. Women, in his judgment, were to be trifled
with, but never seriously consulted; creatures for whom
no flattery was either two high or too low. At the
age of fourteen, the son, certainly with some warrant,
thought to please the father by speaking unfavourably
of that sex ; the only rebuke which he received was a
reminder "from history" that *men* had done much
more mischief; and the child is advised "not to trust
either more than was absolutely necessary." He warns
his son, and his godson afterwards, that they may possibly merit his *aversion;* and that if once he quarrels
with them, he will never forgive. Perhaps one result
of this admonition was that the son married without
his father's consent, leaving a widow and two children.
But Chesterfield's practice was more amiable than his
theory in this instance. If he received Mrs. Eugenia
Stanhope coldly, he treated both her and her boys
with essential kindness; and if he relapsed into the
same severe tone with his godson, it was perhaps

because an old man's language is often less flexible than his heart.

It is wonderful that a man who attributed the infirmities of his age in part to the excesses of his youth should not have been, if not more positive in preventing, at least more guarded against suggesting vice, where the propensities of the young are so apt to take a hint from their elders for the worse. But the truth is that, for all his superior insight, *deteriora sequi* was for him not so much a blemish as a necessity; what men of his rank and degree of culture habitually did was a law of the Medes and Persians which altereth not. His Letters serve a better purpose than that for which he designed them; they are a standing evidence of the danger of that common theory which regards certain vices as inevitable. Carefully as he watched his son's career, there was one part of the temptations to which youth is exposed, in which he sometimes gave a general encouragement to evil, whilst as to particular instances he deliberately and avowedly remained in ignorance. He calls him in one place, but with not the slightest evidence of censure, a dissipated young man of twenty; yet it is clear that the lad's leading propensity was to study; his father is manifestly alarmed lest his education in the manners and graces, in which he was certainly sadly lacking, should be further impeded by his devotion to his book, and it is, therefore, all the more remarkable that he should have chosen for his governor the Rev. Mr. Harte, of whose social qualities Chesterfield thought very little, who was, in fact, if we may infer anything from the manner in which he speaks of him, just one of those awkward scholars upon whom he is never tired of pouring contempt. But the awkwardness of the pupil, whatever it may have been, was not the awkwardness of a stupid lout; Boswell, a most competent observer, remembered him as the Resident at Dresden, and declares that though he could not boast of the graces, he was, in truth, a sensible, civil, well-behaved man. One of his faults is more often found combined with intelligence than with dullness; his father blames him as critical and disputatious; proof that independent observation and study were more to him than parental advice. One instance of this remains : on a set of political precepts which his father had inclosed to him was found written in Philip Stanhope's handwriting, " Excellent maxims, but more calculated for the meridian of France or Spain than of England." It may be that he here puts his finger upon the real defect of a statesmanship rather acute than robust; more sympathetic with foreign than domestic modes of thought, and consequently perhaps more really successful, as it certainly won a greater reputation, in dealing with Irish than with English politics. Chesterfield writes in 1758 : " I am glad you have connected your negotiations and anecdotes ; and, I hope, not with your usual laconism." Laconism, when it is critical, is sometimes a formidable weapon; and he may have had some uncomfortable inklings of its possible strength.

Perhaps we made too much of this one spark from

a small and long-extinguished fire; but it is sometimes given us to guess the general texture of a mind
from a very few threads. At any rate, we cannot help
feeling a little pathetic interest in this somewhat
shadowy figure, whose failings have been registered
amply, and probably with exaggeration; whose troubles,
and perhaps better affections, only come to us through
the refrigerating medium of his father's correspondence; who certainly underwent some humiliations
through the circumstances of his birth; and who, in a
more democratic age, or wherever social and courtly
influences were no bar to intrinsic worth, might have
played, if not a more conspicuous, at least a more
useful and congenial part.

Well read in Latin and Greek, in French, Italian,
and German literature, the son remained a rugged
Englishman to the last. Chesterfield not only wrote
well, but almost thought, in French; his criticism both
of life and letters is on the French model; his English
idiom is tainted from the same source, not, perhaps, so
much from affectation as from mere habit. We can
scarcely turn a page without encountering such Gal-
licisms as—

" The best scholar *of* a gentleman; it is *equal* to
me; your *whole* turns upon the company you keep;
in the public; upon your subject ; profit *of* it ; *of the
one side and of the other ;* the affairs of *its interior ;* to
give the French the change.*"*

Even in the limited intellectual *pabulum* in which
he indulged himself his habitual choice was more

limited still; it is easy to see in what pastures he delighted to feed; thus the statement that "all attentions are repaid, though real obligations are not," is characteristic of a man bred upon Rochefoucauld and Voltaire. The self-sufficiency which so often mars even the best French criticism Chesterfield exhibits in a ludicrous degree. The only Italian poets worth reading are Ariosto and Tasso; Dante, he says, he could never understand, and, *therefore*, had done with him, fully convinced that he was not worth the pains. Of Voltaire's "Siècle de Louis Quatorze," he says that "Weak minds will not like it, even though they do not understand it; which is commonly the measure of their admiration." It would have been well for his own reputation as a critic if he had been guilty of this weakness instead of another weakness still more contemptible. His remarks upon Greek literature are curious and, in their way, instructive, as illustrating both the condition of these studies in his time and the bias of his own mind. As his boy, at the age of sixteen, desired an establishment in England in preference to a foreign appointment, he jocularly suggests that he should become a Greek professor at one of our Universities, a very pretty sinecure, requiring very little knowledge—"much less, I hope, than you have already"—of that language. Greek ought to share some part of every day: not the Greek poets, the "catches" of Anacreon, or the "tender complaints" of Theocritus, or "even the porter-like language of Homer's heroes," but Plato, Aristoteles,

Demosthenes, and Thucydides. Yet of Plato, as of Cicero, he remarks that "It is their eloquence only that has preserved and transmitted them down to us through so many centuries ; for the philosophy of them is wretched, and the reasoning part miserable."

This being his estimate of these great writers, it is not surprising that, at the convenient season, the study of them is put in proper subordination to more serious pursuits. The ruling ambition survives even in our ashes, and as a Cambridge Don of considerable classical acquirements, but also a good cricketer in his day, is said to have declared, " I would rather hit a good smack to leg than write Plato ; " so Chesterfield affirms " I had rather that you were passionately in love with some determined coquette of condition (who would lead you a dance, fashion, supple, and polish you) than that you knew all Plato and Aristotle by heart." An account which he gives of Berkeley's philosophy is, of course, sad rubbish, and it is scarcely necessary to say that he repeats the common cant of the *connoisseur* of his generation about the rude, un-cultivated genius of Shakespeare, whom a better education would have saved "from many extrava-gances and much nonsense." We suspect that he would have said much more to the same purpose if the world had not already made up its mind on the subject. How small a place Shakespeare really had in his thoughts is, perhaps, manifest from a single instance. He has occasion to introduce the Earl of Huntingdon to Madame du Boccage, and he presents

him as a descendant in the direct line of that " Milord
Hastings" who plays so considerable a part in the
tragedy, which the lady has doubtless read, of " Jane
Shore." It is almost impossible not to fret, even when
one laughs, at an egotism so narrow and even stupid
as Chesterfield's about certain departments of culture.
He held music in sovereign contempt, as an occupation quite unfit for a gentleman ; it is not even, like
painting and sculpture, a liberal art, although to his
disgust it is beginning to be thought so.   A gentleman
who loves music will get his piping and fiddling done
for him ; if he does it for himself he puts himself in a
very frivolous and contemptible light.   The vulgariz-
ing effect of such trivial pursuits would, it appears, be
seriously detrimental to the refining influence of the
sedulous endeavours, so religiously inculcated, to break
the Seventh Commandment.   Perhaps we have said
more than enough of the moral shortcomings revealed
in this collection, but we must quote one instance of
social insincerity which a comparison of letters brings
to light.   Madame de Cursay, mother of Madame de
Monconseil, had been seriously ill.   Chesterfield tells
the daughter that his son had informed him of this
circumstance with the keen concern that gratitude
ought to inspire, assures her that he had shared her
justes alarmes, and that he shared also her rejoicing
at the convalescence, "je ne dis pas d'une mère,
mais d'une amie si chère." To his son he writes in
response to the letter telling him of the old lady's
illness :

" If old Cursay goes to the Valley of Jehoshaphat, I cannot help it; it will be an ease to our friend, Madame Monconseil, who, I believe, maintains her, and a little will not satisfy her in any way "

This duplicity is characteristic of the manners of an age which regarded directness and plain honesty of speech as a note of bad breeding; in strong contrast with our own time, when brusqueness is a polite art, and elaborate courtesy is a trifle vulgar. According to Chesterfield only a John Trot would say to a newly-married man, " Sir, I wish you much joy ; " or to a man who has lost a son, " Sir, I am sorry for your loss ; " a well-bred man will advance with warmth, vivacity, and a cheerful countenance to the one, and, embracing him, will say, " If you do justice to my attachment to you, you will judge of the joy that I feel upon this occasion better than I can express it ; " whilst to the other he will adopt a grave composure of countenance and a lower voice, and say, " I hope you do me the justice to be convinced that I feel whatever you feel, and shall ever be affected when you are concerned."

Not only our present manners but our present speech would have seemed vulgar to Chesterfield. We note, after Dr. Bradshaw, that to him "sensible" meant "sensitive," its present use, according to Johnson, being restricted to "low" conversation. Chesterfield apologizes for using the *vulgar* expression, " The will will be taken for the deed." " To be in high spirits " he describes as a silly term then becoming fashionable.

All proverbs and trite sayings, such as " Tit for tat," or " What is one man's meat is another man's poison," he held in special abhorrence. The son is cautioned not to use " namely " because it is Scriptural. Chesterfield would have scorned the man who professed himself *obleiged*, instead of *obleeged* to him. Pronunciation has the ups and downs of two buckets in a well; the vulgarism of one generation is the standard usage of the next, and *vice versâ*. But Chesterfield's authority has prevailed on one point. When Johnson published the " Plan for his Dictionary," he was told by Chesterfield that the word *great* should be pronounced so as to rhyme to *state*, whilst Sir William Yonge affirmed that it should rhyme to *seat*, and that none but an Irishman would pronounce it *grait ;* when, as he says, the best speaker in the House of Lords, and the best speaker in the House of Commons thus differed entirely, the wise lexicographer represented both sounds as equally defensible by authority, and gave instances of both from English verse.

Chesterfield's very limited acquaintance even with the writings of that Augustan age, as it is strangely called, which was well within the range of his life, is strikingly exhibited in his description of *humour*. To him, as to us, the humourist is he who seizes and depicts, not he who is guilty of the absurd or whimsical; and to this effect he writes to some anonymous French lady, in correction of the Abbé le Blanc's " Lettres d'un François " in 1745. We have little doubt that the Abbé derived his notion of the word from a

literature then scarcely more than thirty years old ;
at any rate, he could easily have justified himself from
the " Spectator "—a strange shifting of the point of
view within one generation. From these letters we
discover that "unwell" was in the middle of the
last century an *Irishism*, to describe a middle
state between health and sickness; while many a
careless speaker now may be comforted to know that
the great Chesterfield is guilty of writing " between
you and I."

Narrow as was Chesterfield's scope in the province
of letters, it must in fairness be admitted that upon
his own ground he is often clear-sighted enough. His
criticism of the French writing fashionable in the
middle of the eighteenth century, its affectations, its
neologisms, its quest of *l'esprit, invitâ Minervâ*, is
probably quite just ; like Ixion, he says, such writers
embrace a cloud instead of the goddess they are pursuing ; he was right in preferring to all this the luminous
and effortless precision of Voltaire. He cleverly says
in French of a certain writer of the *galimatias* in
vogue, that—

"God never meant men to think after that fashion, any
more than He meant them to walk on their hands with their
feet in the air, although, by persevering effort, they have
succeeded in doing both the one and the other."

His lucidity and point, unmistakably of French
origin, excited the surprise and admiration, and even
perhaps the genuine envy of the French correspondents
on whom he returned their own native products with

increase; and the same traits frequently enliven his English letters. Count Sinzendorf, for instance, the Imperial Minister, left the Hague one Sunday morning, declaring with an air of mystery that he was going to see some of the province and might possibly go to Spa : " But for my own part," writes Chesterfield to Lord Townshend, " as I know the gentleman, I do not believe the mystery is upon account of the journey, but I rather believe that he takes the journey for the sake of the mystery."

More severe still is his sarcasm on that mad-brained and most uncomfortable creature, the father of Frederick the Great, who made his son swear, among many other things, that he would never believe the doctrine of predestination !   " A very unnecessary declaration," says Chesterfield, " for anybody who has the misfortune of being acquainted with him to make, since Providence can never be supposed to have preordained such a creature ! "

His abilities in this way were more amiably exercised in playing lightly with the infirmities of his old age ; to his well-known *mot*, " Tyrawley and I have been dead these two years, but we do not wish it to be generally known," we might add his willingness to part with his " hereditary right " to deafness " to any Minister to whom hearing is often disagreeable, or to any fine woman, to whom it is often dangerous."   In spite of his own urgent advice, " abstain carefully from satire," it is impossible that he could have kept this dangerous power constantly under control ; and there is probably some truth in Lord Hervey's statement that "from his propensity to ridicule he was rather liked than loved."

When Chesterfield proposed a certain name to George II., and the monarch angrily said, "I would rather have the devil," the Minister reminded him that the personage he preferred must be addressed in the commission as "our trusty and well-beloved cousin." George may have laughed, but we have a suspicion that the ready humour here displayed was not always really acceptable to a king in whose composition, according to Chesterfield, everything was little, who loved to act the king but mistook the part, and in whom the Royal dignity shrunk into the Electoral pride. It is to Chesterfield's honour, perhaps, that in spite of his acknowledged grace of manner he was not successful as a courtier. He avowed a profound mistrust of George II., based, it may be, in part upon those conversations, in which he affirms the character of kings is best discovered. He imputes to him the same treachery which stained the greater name of Marlborough; he more than insinuates that the failure of the expedition to Brest was brought about by Court intrigue; and speaks of the *bugbear* of a French invasion, kept alive, he says, regardless of grammar, by "I know who, and I know why." Great as were his own merits as a politician, he was able to despise, but unable to dispense with some of the practices of a corrupt time; he writes that "his son will be brought into Parliament without opposition, but not *gratis;*" and ten years later he assists in a negotiation by which the young man, who, as resident in an official position abroad, could not possibly have discharged his duty as a member of the House of Commons, is to vacate his seat "for a valuable consideration, meaning *money*." This more than acquiescence in certain arrangements as necessary evils is characteristic of the man; and we trace at once cynicism and irony in his style when, in attempting to give some notion of the delays and absurd difficulties that arose in a negotiation with the United Provinces—

"Represent to yourself," he writes, "an *English* Minister endeavouring to carry a point by the single merit of the point itself, without the assistance of reward and punishments, through what patriots would call an independent and unbiassed House of Commons—that is, an assembly of people influenced by everything but by the Court, and then judge how soon and how easily it would pass!"

He himself suffered by the methods which he here describes. In 1732 he opposed Walpole's Excise scheme, and was in consequence deprived of his white staff; yet at a later date he recommends to Newcastle vindictive proceedings of much the same kind as the only way to secure a stable administration. On the topic of clemency there is indeed a strange incongruity between Chesterfield's language on various occasions, due rather to the fact that, whether through conviction or prejudice, the circumstances seemed to him to be radically different, than to any vicissitudes in a temper so controlled and equable as his. His mild but firm

administration of Ireland was marred by no trepida-
tion. He was told one morning that the people of
Connaught were rising. He took out his watch and
said simply, " It is nine o'clock, and certainly time for
them to rise." Yet at the very same date he was
using, with respect to the rebels in Scotland, language
so savage that if we did not know the man we should
certainly attribute it to the anger which not uncom-
monly goes hand in hand with panic. Had the
" Butcher" Cumberland been under his instructions he
might fairly have pleaded that he had not exceeded
them. " Let the Duke put all to fire and sword."
" The Commander-in-Chief should be ordered to give
no quarter, but to pursue and destroy the rebels
wherever he finds them." So wrote a wise and sym
pathetic ruler, who in his general correspondence exhibits a disgust, then uncommon among statesmen,
even at such horrors as are inevitable in any form of
warfare.

Chesterfield's Lord-Lieutenancy was of brief dura-
tion, and from it we cannot discover how far he would
have been able to grapple with immediate public
dangers, which never in fact troubled him during his
stay in Ireland. His interest in that country did not
terminate with his office, and he was wont, on the
strength of his Lieutenancy, to call himself an Irishman ; he maintained a constant correspondence upon
Irish affairs with Dr. Chenevix, Bishop of Waterford,
(who had formerly been his chaplain at the Hague), with
Mr. Thomas Prior, and with Alderman Faulkner, a

F

gentleman who answers exactly to Mr. Boffin's description of Mr. Silas Wegg as "a literary party with a wooden leg."[1] At times Chesterfield's tone in these letters is more cheerful than we could have anticipated; and did we not remember how low was his estimate of our English education, especially at Westminster, then perhaps our representative school, we should be surprised at his conviction that the state of schools and of university education in Ireland was better than ours; just as we stumble at his more general declaration, made, it is true, at a time of great national despondency here, that the prospects of Ireland were more *hopeful* than those of England! But Cassandra is never long absent from the elbow of the Irish historian or statesman. The extravagance and dissipation which Chesterfield regretted in 1746 Burke was still regretting fifty years later: "Except in your claret," writes Chesterfield, "which you are very solicitous should be two or three years old, you think less of two or three years hence than any people under the sun."

With a laudable zeal to promote Irish industries, he urges the manufacture of glass bottles : " Considering," he says, "the close connection there is between bottles and claret, I should hope that this manufacture, *though your own*, may meet with encouragement." He suggests that every Irishman should make as many

---

[1] This leg Foote had the inhumanity to ridicule upon the stage. He was properly punished by an accident which led to the amputation of his own.

bottles as he empties. He was keenly alive to the mischiefs of civil disabilities for the Irish Romanists ; and would have them tied down "by the tender but strong bonds of landed property." But his great merit is that he saw the necessity of moral as well as mechanical reform ; and it is this insight that prompts him to exclaim, " When Ireland is no longer dependent upon England, the Lord have mercy upon it." If we regret that with him, as with most politicians of his day, the peasantry of Ireland are much in the background, we must note at the same time his declaration, when the Whiteboys in 1764 had been troublesome, that " if the military force had killed half as many landlords it would have contributed more effectually to restore quiet."[1]   At a time when the Lord-Lieutenants were generally governed by the dominant faction, and secured their own peace and ignoble ease by keeping that satisfied, he resolved " to take trouble upon himself," and haughtily refused to be the " first slave " of a set of unscrupulous and greedy placemen.   If expediency led him to insist on the dangers to Ireland of " starting points which ought never to have been mentioned at all," his determination to see things with his own eyes marks one of the best elements in his character.   He had, besides, that cosmopolitan temper, so much needed, and yet so lamentably wanting in our past treatment of the Irish

[1] He adds : " The poor people in Ireland are used worse than negroes by their lords and masters, and their deputies of deputies of deputies."

problem. His contempt of the pride of birth was no pretence ; and he was certainly equally exempt from the pride of race. In one sense the most aristocratic of aristocrats, good society meant for him not necessarily well-born, but always well-bred and accomplished people ; and his strict inculcation of courtesy to servants and inferiors was part of a humane spirit, which acknowledged no natural inferiority, whether of social *status*[1] or of nationality. He notices with censure the contempt of historians for humanity in general, and no Socialist orator in Trafalgar Square could more strongly denounce the ambition of crowned heads, whose principal business, according to him, was the extermination of their fellow-creatures. When he waxes hot upon this theme he sometimes sacrifices truth to epigram. " Happy were it for England," he exclaims, "happy for the world, if there were not great kings in it," forgetting that the weakness of monarchs has caused at least as great miseries as their power.

Of his prescience much has been written. He saw, long before a storm was suspected, the cloud small as a man's hand which was to gather into the French Revolution. He guessed the incapacity which, at least for many generations, the French people exhibited for Constitutional government. " Vous savez faire des barricades mais vous n'élèverez jamais des barrières,"

---

[1] Occasional expressions notwithstanding. " Gout," he says, "is the distemper of a gentleman, whereas the rheumatism is the distemper of a hackney-coachman or chairman."

he says in words which read rather like history than prophecy. He foretold the extinction of the temporal power of the Papacy; yet to long-sighted people things remote are often more visible than things near, and on the eve of England's second heroic age he seems to have had scarcely any suspicion of the commanding genius of Pitt, whom nevertheless he helped to his brilliant ascendancy. He was an able diplomatist, and these letters would enable us, if we had space, to give detailed instances of his skill. He did not disdain to bring his social qualities into the game ; and often by means of *badinage* discovered some things which he wanted to know. His methods of policy were in every direction quiet and unobtrusive ; thus he boasts that it was his resignation of the Secretaryship of State that *made* the peace of Aix-la-Chapelle, by opening people's eyes to the imminent dangers of the war. He had the invaluable art of concealing his ignorance with dexterity ; his most famous achievement is per- haps the reform of the Calendar, yet he declares that of all the substantial part of his brilliant speech upon that measure he did not himself understand a word. Long before his decease he wrote as one for whom the idle dream of this world was over ; yet he emerged from his obscurity to urge with success upon the king that alliance between Pitt and Newcastle, which was the first step to the restoration of our *prestige* abroad through a series of glorious triumphs by land and sea. A safe reputation such as his has a peculiar fascina- tion, because it leaves so much room for conjecture.

More adventurous characters give the historian many more topics for praise or blame, but the colours in which they are painted are fast and clear, and speculation is displaced by some positive judgment where men have done all that it was possible for them to do. The Chesterfields of politics leave us problems none the less interesting because they are insoluble; and we are constantly asking, though with no prospect of reply, whether their reserve was due to self-knowledge or to magnanimity, and whether, if they would, they could have achieved more.

ARNOLD'S ESSAYS IN CRITICISM

SECOND SERIES

I T is not too soon to try to estimate Matthew Arnold's work as a critic. Long before his too early death he had done for us all he could. He had given vogue to modes of thought and judgment which were once rare amongst Englishmen. He would have disclaimed, with some repugnance, the suggestion that he had a method. But if he had not a method, he had a mystery, an open secret, the habit of seeing every object before him in a perspective of wide culture and observation. He taught us to have this aim, and, given the requisite breadth and knowledge—

> "Most can raise the flower now
> For all have got the seed."

That "World Literature" which was the dream of Goethe, a literature exempt from the prejudices and eccentricities which national isolation begets, and always making mute appeal to a tribunal, if not cosmopolitan at least European, has through Matthew Arnold become more possible for us. In many cases, therefore, it became easy to foresee *what* Matthew

Arnold would say, if not exactly *how* he would say it. But there was, besides, in his criticism a personal element against which, for a thoroughly just judgment, it is always necessary to be on our guard. It gave him currency, it made him delightfully readable ; we would not have missed it for the world. Let it amuse us ; "we are none of us," he would himself say, "likely to be lively much longer," and some of the gaiety of criticism is already eclipsed with him. But let us remember that wherever this personal element appears there is no longer the single eye, and the mark is not always hit.

In one direction, indeed, this personal element covered a very large extent of ground. He claimed for culture an empire which it never could achieve without a complete change of character. He had, we believe, a sincere sympathy with the devoted labourer in the work of social reformation, but he often dissembled his love, and, to a world oblivious of nice distinctions, he seemed like a well-dressed stranger criticising the workman in the gravel-pit below for the inevitable soils and tatters of his clothes. The motto which Mr. Frederic Harrison has chosen for his dialogue on "Culture" :

> "The sovereign'st thing on earth
> Was parmaceti for an inward bruise,"

suggested a picture, consolatory to the wounded feelings of many a Hotspur in the battle of life. We take up Matthew Arnold's last volume and we light upon this :

"The 'scientific system of thought' in Wordsworth gives us at last such poetry as this, which the devout Wordsworthian accepts :

> 'O for the coming of that glorious time
> When, prizing knowledge as her noblest wealth
> And best protection, this Imperial Realm,
> While she exacts allegiance, shall admit
> An obligation, on her part, to *teach*
> Them who are born to serve her and obey ;
> Binding herself by statute to secure,
> For all the children whom her soil maintains,
> The rudiments of letters, and inform
> The mind with moral and religious truth.'

Wordsworth calls Voltaire dull, and surely the production of these un-Voltairian lines must have been imposed on him as a judgment ! One can hear them being quoted at a Social Science Congress; one can call up the whole scene. A great room in one of our dismal provincial towns ; dusty air and jaded afternoon daylight ; benches full of men with bald heads and women in spectacles ; an orator lifting up his face from a manuscript written within and without to declaim these lines of Wordsworth ; and in the soul of any poor child of nature who may have wandered in thither, an unutterable sense of lamentation, and mourning, and woe ! "

Now this is amusing, and possibly true and admirable, as a piece of literary criticism ; but would not any one who did not know the writer and the field of survey which he claimed for himself, suppose that we had here a fastidious *æsthete*, a spirit altogether too delicate, too much impressed by external uncomeliness, to deal with questions of moral evil at all ?

Alas ! the centres of so much moral ugliness are apt
to be themselves ugly, ⸾and too much working or
thinking about these things commonly ends in bald
heads and spectacles ; but to serious minds, who remember that poetry is often stimulating and fruitful
out of all proportion to its æsthetic merit, Matthew
Arnold's criticism upon this particular passage of
Wordsworth will inevitably, to the obscuring of all
that he really wishes to convey, suggest the reflection
that what with the children of nature whom he desires
to multiply and the children of nature who multiply
themselves only too fast, bald heads and spectacles
are likely to be on the increase among us.   We must
add that if, as Matthew Arnold is never tired of telling
us, literature is " a criticism of life " ; if " the strongest
part of our religion to-day is its unconscious poetry " ;
if we are one day to learn to say, " Poetry is the
reality, philosophy the illusion," the province of poetry
is by these propositions made so wide, the task committed to her so enormous, and all her extant ap-
paratus so insufficient for her pressing needs, that even
the inferior parts of her workmanship which find
favour with "'those bold bad men,' the haunters of
social science congresses," will prove very serviceable.
But the truth is that the propositions of enormous
reach, which the great critic was accustomed to use, are
many of them unworkable dogmas, at many points
more demonstrably false than the articles of any
theological creed. He has contrasted literature and
dogma; but literature herself abounds in dogmas, which

are only saved from sceptical attack because too much is not at present claimed for them. "Beauty is truth ; truth beauty," says Keats ; and we accept this now as a stimulating and fruitful saying, giving a worthy aim to men's efforts in art or letters, fixing men's eyes upon remote but glorious possibilities, and perhaps suggesting the faith that in some sphere beyond our present ken the identity is already complete. But conceive this bright fancy, so potent whilst it is left at large in the province of the imagination, yet so absolutely dogmatic in form, urged as a rule for the practical guidance of life, and proclaimed by the high priests of culture in all the churches of the future as "the serious one thing needful"; and what a revolt against it there will be among poor mortals, who can never be long oblivious of tangible or historic facts! Truth is often ugly ; beauty is often illusion ; these are counter-propositions which can scarcely be denied even by the most transcendental mind. Inoperative now, what powerful solvents they will then be, in combination with the fear, not unwarranted by experience, that beauty accepted for truth may mean for fallible and impressionable men grace without morals ! And the refinements and distinctions, however just and true, by which these objections may be obviated, will inevitably seem to be at least as sophistical and far-fetched as the subtleties of any theologian in defence or explanation of some doubtful and difficult text.

Matthew Arnold,[1] criticising a passage from

---

[1] Mixed Essays. A French Critic on Milton.

Macaulay's Essay on Milton, says of it, "Substantial meaning such lucubrations have none." We are almost inclined to thank him for teaching us that word. The passage to which he applies it is indeed painfully rhetorical, and, after the manner of youthful rhetoricians, precision is sacrificed to rhetoric. The statement that "Milton wrote in an age of philosophers and theologians" implies a distinction between Milton and Dante, which, apart from the context, is wholly misleading. Such antitheses as "the material or immaterial system," "philosophically in the wrong, but poetically in the right," betray the ambitious but inexperienced penman. So we have written; and the words shall stand, as an evidence how far implicit trust in Matthew Arnold may betray us. We must be on our guard, he tells us, against the devout Wordsworthians. We must be on our guard, experience proves, against the antagonists of Macaulay. Vulnerable as he is, he has assuredly some protecting genius who smites *them* with obliquity of vision at the moment of attack. One accuses him of bad scholarship, and makes a gross blunder in grammar in a familiar passage of Greek. Another sets him right about Claverhouse, and begins by giving Claverhouse the wrong Christian name. Another accuses him of garbling, and leaves off a crucial passage in the middle. And here we have Matthew Arnold charging him with no meaning, and omitting from the words which he adduces to prove his charge every indication of their real purport. To use a vulgar but expressive figure of speech the passage has been simply "*gutted.*" It is, as we discover at once on turning to the essay itself, Johnson who is really responsible for the antithesis between the "material" and the "immaterial system." He says, "the poet should have secured the consistency of his system by keeping immateriality out of sight, and seducing the reader to drop it from his thoughts." To which Macaulay in effect replies that this was impossible; that the tendencies, the modes of thought belonging to Milton's time, forbade it; that a sort of compromise was necessary, if the poet was to engage "that half-belief, which poetry requires." Matthew Arnold cites with approval M. Scherer's *dictum* that "the fundamental conceptions of *Paradise Lost* have become foreign to us." Well, Macaulay's *dictum* is that Dante's conceptions of the spiritual world had become foreign to the age of Milton. Why is the one *dictum* wisdom and the other foolishness?

On the other hand, Matthew Arnold himself is constantly offering us the semblance of thoughts which dissolve into airy nothings the moment we attempt to give them "substantial meaning":

"Our religion has materialized itself in the fact, the supposed fact; it has attached its emotion to the fact, and now the fact is failing it. But for poetry the idea is everything; the rest is a world of illusion, of divine illusion. Poetry attaches its emotion to the idea; the idea is the fact. The strongest part of our religion to-day is its unconscious poetry."

How can we help retorting here that this is sheer
nonsense; that "substantial meaning such lucubrations
have none "?   " Our religion has materialized itself in
the fact." Assuredly this implies a gradual deteriora-
tion ; an undue prominence given, in process of time,
to the fact, as compared with the ideas which the fact
may be supposed to symbolize. The historic truth, of
course, is that our religion from the very first, and
then most ardently, " attached its emotion to the fact "
or "the supposed fact." But for this it would have had
no existence. The disease, if disease it is, is congenital ;
nay, the very life of " our religion " (if by " our religion "
is meant Christianity) has been one " long disease."
This is so obvious that we are forced to suppose that
" our religion " means something less determinate—is,
in fact, another name for the religious emotions of
mankind, which, in as far as they are distinctively
Christian, have been " materialized." But then, " the
strongest part of our religion to-day is its unconscious
poetry." " Its *unconscious* poetry," observe ; that
poetry effortless, spontaneous, which flourishes everywhere in an atmosphere of beautiful legend, accepted
with implicit belief. But so little is this unconscious
poetry independent of the fact—that is, of course, of
belief in the fact—that when " the fact fails it," in
plain English when men cease to believe their legends,
their poetry is no longer unconscious, no longer
intensely emotional, no longer in any proper sense
religious. They pass consciously from belief to make-
believe, and Matthew Arnold would fain tempt us to

take make-believe for belief. But "surely in vain is this net spread in the sight of any bird." The poetry for which "the idea is everything," the poetry which is content to take the idea for the fact, when the fact fails it, may have every quality save one ; but it has no religion in it. It may add much to the refinement of life, but it has little controlling power over conscience or conduct. The emotions which it excites are altogether too superficial, too consciously æsthetic or artistic, too much the result of a deliberate surrender to illusion, to supply motive or principle. If these are truisms, so much the worse for the vague but pretentious generalities which the mere statement of truisms can explode. "The house is falling about your ears ; but never mind, it is still to all intents and purposes a commodious mansion, for you can still make a picture of it," is scarcely a parody of the sweet and reasonable message which, in this and similar passages, the Apostle of Culture conveys to the Christian world.

And then that talk about "a world of illusion, of divine illusion," surely, as he would himself say, "imposed" upon the contemner of philosophy "as a judgment"—the abstract character, without the method, of metaphysics ; the voice the voice of a cautious and discerning Jacob, but the hands the hands of a wild and rambling Esau, gathering from all quarters his incongruous spoil ! That the phenomenal world is a world of divine illusion, we are quite prepared to believe ; albeit it is an opinion which certainly owes its acceptance to the philosophy which we are told is probably itself illusive. What else there is anywhere which can properly be called "divine illusion," we are unable to conceive. We know no sense in which the illusion, whatever it may be which belongs to the world of human thought and emotion, can be said to be divine. Yet what is "the rest" of which Matthew Arnold speaks above, if not the whole world of nature and human life, exclusive of the ideas which poetry thence gathers? Definition, indeed, is as difficult as respiration in these high latitudes; what Barrow says of wit is in place here— we might as well attempt "to make a portrait of Proteus, or to define the figure of the fleeting air." "We must take," as Macaulay would say, "what meaning we can get and be thankful." Or, better, we must take concrete instances, and try to gain from these some interpretation of a language at present too much in the void. The Ariels of literature will, of course, protest against any Philistine Sycorax who attempts to fasten them thus as "within a cloven pine." But they can expect no deliverer, if they are thus fixed, not for refusing to serve us, but for pretending to be executing supernatural ministries, while they are only carrying out earthly behests. We open upon a passage like this in the same essay from which we made our last quotation :

"The world of Chaucer is fairer, richer, more significant than that of Burns ; but when the largeness and freedom of Burns get full sweep, as in 'Tam o' Shanter,' or, still more,

in that puissant and splendid production 'The Jolly Beggars,' his world may be what it will, his poetic genius
triumphs over it. In the world of 'The Jolly Beggars'
there is more than hideousness and squalor, there is bes-
tiality; yet the piece is a superb poetical success. It has
breadth, truth, and power which made the famous scene in
Auerbach's cellar, of Goethe's 'Faust,' seem artificial and
tame beside it."

Τί ταῦτα πρὸς Διόνυσον; what have these things to do
with those solemn words which seemed to announce a
new *cultus*? Poetry, superb poetry, sublimated out of
a coarse and bestial life—the thing is, we suppose,
conceivable to the æsthetic mind which knows nothing
of moral scruples, and whether in Murillo's " Beggar
Boys" or in Burns's " Jolly Beggars" is prepared to
praise the efficient rendering of dirt ; but what a
transition we have made in the space of a few pages !
We seemed to have passed, as the traveller in Italy
passes, through the portico of a ruined temple into a
hovel. It is not enough to reply that the transition
is delicately managed ; that Matthew Arnold has
previously told us that Burns's moralizing lacks that
" accent of high seriousness, born of absolute sincerity,"
which we find in Dante. For all this, he too clearly
shows us that the image of his idolatry has feet of clay.
For, given that with "high seriousness" or without it,
on themes the most exalted and themes the most
sordid and vile, superb poetry is possible ; and what is
the inference? Clearly that the imaginative faculty
may select and glorify, but does not create the elements

G

which give to poetry whatever of moral force she possesses, and that where moral fibre is wanting, it is not in poetry to supply it.

Matthew Arnold indeed betrays some uneasy consciousness of a truth so obvious that a criticism so comprehensive as his could not fail to encounter the proofs of it at a thousand points. Voltaire has said that " no nation has treated in poetry moral ideas with more energy and depth than the English nation." And our critic begins by telling us, what few will need to be told, that Voltaire " does not mean by ' treating in poetry moral ideas ' the composing moral and didactic poems." Certainly not ; but between this and the next stage there is perhaps more than one halting-place which he passes unnoticed. For Voltaire means, it appears, " the noble and profound application of ideas to life." Whether Voltaire, among whose deficiencies we cannot reckon a want of lucidity, would have accepted this amplification of a meaning, perfectly intelligible if his words are taken in their ordinary sense ; whether this is not one of several instances of a tantalizing trick, practised by Matthew Arnold to perfection, by which the more nebulous notions of to-day are read into the clear, if limited, thinking of a previous age, we shall better see as we proceed :

" He means the application of these ideas under the conditions fixed for us by the laws of poetic beauty and poetic truth. If it is said that to call these ideas *moral* ideas is to introduce a strong and injurious limitation, I answer that it is to do nothing of the kind, because moral ideas are really so main a part of human life. The question, *How to live*, is itself a moral idea, and it is the question which most interests every man, and with which, in some way or other, he is perpetually occupied. A large sense is, of course, to be given to the term *moral*. Whatever bears upon the question, ' How to live ' comes under it :

> ' Nor love thy life, nor hate ; but, what thou liv'st
> Live well; how long or short, permit to heaven.'

In those fine lines Milton utters, as every one at once perceives, a moral idea. Yes, but so too, when Keats consoles the forward-bending lover on the Grecian Urn, the lover arrested and presented in immortal relief by the sculptor's hand before he can kiss, with the line :

> ' For ever wilt thou love, and she be fair—'

he utters a moral idea. When Shakespeare says that—

> ' We are such stuff
> As dreams are made of, and our little life
> Is rounded with a sleep,—'

he utters a moral idea."

" Every one perceives " that there is a moral idea in the third of these quotations scarcely less obvious than that of the first. But observe how comfortably the passage in which it is difficult to find any suggestion which can be reasonably called moral, is " sandwiched " between the first and third. That line of Keats an example of the kind of thing Voltaire meant when he spoke of the English treatment of moral ideas in poetry! The notion is almost grotesque. There is nothing, we may be sure, in the whole of the "Ode on a Grecian Urn," which he would have called either distinctively moral or distinctively English. Even if we use the term moral in the "large sense" which we are expected to give to it, we are puzzled to discover in what way the words,

"For ever wilt thou love, and she be fair,"

bear upon the question, "how to live." We are only conscious that we have been presented with a monster balloon of theory, and that our morality is expected to become gaseous in order to inflate it.

We may be thought to have given a disproportionate treatment to the ethical side of Matthew Arnold's criticism. Yet we have certainly not given it more consideration than he would expect for it, and if we were free to discuss it at much further length, he supplies us with abundant material. His intellectual convictions and his moral sympathies had made an armistice which he persuaded himself, and tried to persuade the world, might be the basis of a lasting peace. But habits of mind such as his end legitimately in Renan, and only anomalously in Matthew Arnold. A not unkindly Nemesis made this great enemy of anomalies and provincialism himself an anomaly peculiarly insular and English. This son of religious England could never "forget his own people and his father's house," and was quite incapable of the frank, if regretful, abandonment of earlier pre-

possessions which brought his French contemporary
to the spiritual condition of the Parisian *gamin*. He
put himself therefore in that middle place " to God and
to His enemies alike displeasing," which to be tenable
required either more faith or less. He never realized
what Renan well knew, that the word " illusion!" is a
baneful spell, which, for the soul that has learned to
utter it, reduces the beautiful form and voice of religion
to a gibbering phantom. He never patiently thought
things out in these greatest questions of the present
and future; and the effect—if it is not the cause—
is that he believed it possible to keep without vital
inconsistency, and the consequent despondency or
cynicism, the head with the Goethes and Heines and
George Sands, and the whole world of modern pagans,
and the heart with the saints. It was a freak of later
Greek sculpture to combine the face of Hermes with
the thews and sinews of Hercules. This *bizarre* fancy
has more than one parallel among the eccentricities of
modern thought.

Matthew Arnold found no pleasure in the new-
fangled substitutes for religion. Having tasted the old
wine he did not desire the new; he said (but with the
air of a connoisseur licensed to find fault) " the old is
better." His fault-finding however must be admitted,
even by those who admire him most, to be occasionally
very random and slipshod work. Here is a palpable
instance :

" ' Duty exists,' says Wordsworth, in the ' Excursion ' ;
and then he proceeds thus :

'. . . . Immutably survive,
For our support, the measures and the forms,
Which an abstract Intelligence supplies,
Whose kingdom is, where time and space are not.'

And the Wordsworthian is delighted, and thinks that here is a sweet union of philosophy and poetry. But the disinterested lover of poetry will feel that the lines carry us really not a step farther than the proposition which they would interpret ; that they are a tissue of elevated but abstract verbiage, alien to the very nature of poetry."

We will let " the disinterested lover of poetry " say what he pleases about these lines in their poetic character ; nor is this the place to defend them as a fragment of philosophy. But the news that they add nothing to our notions of human obligation is too good to be true ; we should like some other security for this than our critic's autocratic extravagance of speech. He has had much to do, in his quality of critic, with people who found a basis for duty less immutable than that proposed by Wordsworth ; and these people were not always to his taste. " What a set ! What a world ! " he exclaims of the sordid, vapouring, irresponsible company into which poor Shelley threw himself. It is just the sort of comment which was needed ; in these days how thankful we ought to be for a critic, and that one of the greatest of critics, who is capable of these instincts of repulsion and has the courage to express them in a word, conscious though we may be that proximity has something to do with this aversion, and that the shock which is acute when it comes from

quarters so near home, is slight enough from the longi-
tude of Paris or Weimar. But assuredly Matthew
Arnold did not owe to literature, or even " culture,"
his power to resist the glamour with which literature
too often invests questionable morals ; and even his
prejudice in favour of " manners, tone, dignity," belongs
to wholesome traditions the place of which génius
itself cannot supply. His last volume contains some
of his most characteristic work, but we hesitate to say,
with his editor, " his best." His best and surest work
in criticism was his earliest ; the very best of all is
perhaps to be found in his verse. But that is often
most interesting which is least faultless ; and these
last essays of his graceful pen, in spite of the many
instances they afford of personal preference, trying
with but partial success to base itself on principle, will
be welcome to all who have enough freedom of mind
to be fascinated even by the eccentricities of a rarely
gifted spirit.

EDMUND WALLER

THAT Waller revolutionized English poetry is neither a new nor a true discovery. It was announced as long ago as 1690 in a Preface to the second part of his poems, attributed with every probability to Atterbury. Here we find it stated that Waller "was the first that showed us our tongue had beauty and numbers in it." Here we read that he was the first to correct what has, in these latter days, been called the "overflow" in heroic verse. The verses of the men before his time, we are told—

"Ran all into one another, and hung together, throughout a whole copy, like the hooked atoms that compose a body in Des Cartes. There was no distinction of parts, no regular stops, nothing for the ear to rest upon; but as soon as the copy began, down it went like a larum incessantly; and the reader was sure to be out of breath before he got to the end of it; so that really verse, in those days, was but downright prose tagged with rhymes. Mr. Waller removed all these faults, brought in more polysyllables and smoother measures, bound up his thoughts better, and in a cadence more agreeable to the nature of the verse he wrote in; so that wherever the natural stops of that were, he contrived the little breakings of his sense so as to fall in with them."

This is Atterbury, as we conceive of him ; dogmatic
and lucid; but too little painstaking to be exact.
Waller's praise was sung with more discrimination by
Dryden, in 1699. He says indeed that "our numbers
were in their nonage until Waller and Denham
appeared." But in the same valuable document, the
Preface to his Tales, he writes that the "learned and
ingenious Sandys" was—

"The best versifier of the former age : if I may properly
call it by that name, which was the former part of this con-
cluding century. For Spenser and Fairfax both flourished
in the reign of Queen Elizabeth : great masters in our
language : and who saw much farther into the beauties of
our numbers than those who immediately followed them.
Milton was the poetical son of Spenser, and Waller of
Fairfax ; for we have our lineal descents and clans, as well
as other families. Spenser more than once insinuates that
the soul of Chaucer was transfused into his body, and that
he was begotten by him 200 years after his decease. Milton
has acknowledged to me that Spenser was his original;
and many besides myself have heard our famous Waller
own that he derived the harmony of his numbers from the
Godfrey of Bulloigne, which was turned into English by Mr.
Fairfax."

In 1620, when Waller was but fourteen, "the learned
and ingenious Mr. Sandys" had written lines which, if
we modernize the spelling, we might easily pass off
upon the unwary reader as Pope's heroics. And in
spite of Pope's obligations to the large genius of
Dryden, it is to his early delight in Sandys's translation

of the Metamorphoses that he owed that ease and
harmony of numbers which was his from first to last.
Indeed, though he declared that "he had learnt versi-
fication wholly from Dryden's works," it is certain
that there was in Dryden's form much that he could
not, and more that he would not, imitate. This is a
question which any reader may determine for himself.
The ear which has grown accustomed to the smooth
heroics, whether of Waller or of Pope, is conscious of a
régime less precise in the structure of Dryden's lines,
the licence of his rhymes, the frequency of his triplets
and Alexandrines.   In fact, though Pope tells us that

> " Dryden taught to join
> The varying verse, the full resounding line,
> The long majestic march, and energy divine,"

to be strictly accurate, there was much of this which
Dryden could not *teach;* gifts native, individual, in-
communicable, which cannot be formulated, and which
have little to do with the *technique* and mechanism of
poetry.   But if ever any process was inevitable when
once the utility of that form of verse for the treatment
of particular themes was recognized, it was the development of the heroic couplet into the shape which we
know, with something more than satiety, as characteristic of eighteenth-century literature.   In attributing so
much to Waller, Atterbury (perhaps even Dryden to
some extent) is influenced by the overwhelming
ascendancy which this measure had already achieved ;
it pervaded literature for him and clouded the past.

In an age the horizon of which had been narrowed by domestic conflict, an age in which the present was all-engrossing, it had become the characteristic form of serious poetry, the weapon of satire ; of religious and political controversy, in which verse was enlisted, to an extent hitherto unknown ; it had even for a while usurped the tragic stage and those remoter topics, such as Cowley's Davideis, in which the vexed human spirit sought a refuge from the pressure of realities in ideal scenes. One great independent soul, dwelling apart like a star, was above the reach of the prevailing epidemic. The homage of the Tory High Churchman Atterbury for the Republican Puritan Milton is in it-self a charming incongruity ; but it loses none of its fascination by the manner in which it is displayed. He commends Milton's phrase "the troublesome bondage of rhyming"; he points to Milton's triumphant use of freedom ; he hopes for "some excellent spirit to arise that has leisure enough, and resolution to break the charm" under which poetry is at present laid. "But this," he adds, "is a thought for times at some distance. The present age is a little too war-like : it may perhaps furnish out matter for a good poem in the next, but it will hardly encourage one now. Without prophesying, a man may easily know what sort of laurels are like to be in request." All this is excellently said ; and betrays some inkling of the truth that circumstances, rather than individual choice, determine the fashions, as well as the persons that come to the front in literature from time to time.

"The present age is too warlike"; the experiment
required peace, leisure, security ; a mind not absorbed
in the things of the hour.   It is clear that, though he
mentions with praise the meagre and inefficient efforts
of Roscommon in blank verse, he has here in mind its
fitness for some far larger achievement.   Yet how
strangely this comes after a regret that *Waller* never
adopted it!   Rhyme, Atterbury says, must, whether
it will or no, take its place among the things which
Cicero called *lepida et concinna*, which *cito satietate
afficiunt aurium sensum fastidiosissimum :*

"This Mr. Waller understood very well ; and, therefore,
to take off the danger of a surfeit that way, strove to please
by variety and new sounds.   Had he carried this observation,
among others, as far as it would go, it must, methinks, have
shown him the incurable fault of this jingling kind of poetry,
and have led his later judgment to blank verse ; but he
continued an obstinate lover of rhyme to the very last ; it
was a mistress that never appeared unhandsome in his eyes,
and was courted by him long after Sacharissa had been for-
saken."

Why did it not occur to Atterbury, when he was
saying this so prettily, that it was just because Waller's
province was the *lepida et concinna* that rhyme was
his fittest instrument ?   A Waller without rhyme is as
inconceivable as a "Paradise Lost" with it.   His most
serious thoughts are shaped in pretty fancies, seldom
without a touch of epigram.   He carefully nursed his
somewhat slender stock of these.   But whether he
writes in his earlier days to his Amoret—

> "And as pale sickness does invade
> Your frailer part, the breaches made
> In that fair lodging, will more clear
> Make the bright guest, your soul, appear"—

or whether, in old age, without a compliment, and with more of the sad earnestness of a truth felt as well as seen, he pens with trembling hand the words which we all know :

> "The soul's dark cottage, battered and decayed,
> Lets in new light, through chinks that time has made"—

it is surely impossible not to acknowledge that thus and no otherwise could the thing have been said, considering the thought itself, the times, and the man.

The assumed archaism of Spenser and Fairfax, like the real archaism of Chaucer, obscured in the seventeenth century the truth that more had been achieved already in the way of melodious verse, than that or the succeeding century could hope to rival. In Dryden's "Preface," Waller is the poetical son of Fairfax, and could we but disabuse our minds of the notion that the history of methodized verse is the history of the heroic couplet, this pedigree would at once dispose of the view which makes Waller, whose mind was carried, with movements as smooth and facile as his verse, along the stream of circumstance, the author of a sort of poetical *coup d'état*. It is known now that to all intents and purposes the heroic couplet had been brought to a high degree of perfection by Chaucer about 250 years before Waller had written a line ; it

is one of Dryden's venial errors that he did not
acknowledge this, although he admitted that "they
who lived with Chaucer, and some time after him,
thought him musical," and that "he who published
the last edition of him would make us believe the
fault is in our ears, and that there were really ten
syllables in a verse where we find but nine." This
was, in fact, a weapon once bright and keen, which
had grown rusty in the poetical armoury for want of
frequent use. The great masters of harmony among
the Elizabethans had neglected it ; having, we believe,
a truer insight into its limitations than most of their
successors. The truth is that *without* the *enjambement* or "overflow" rhymed heroics are a *bondage ;*
and *with* it they are to many readers now the least
pleasant to the ear of all the well-known forms of
verse. Surely though we may read with some sympathy the protest of Keats against what he calls—

"A schism
Nurtured by foppery and barbarism,"

and the folk who—

"Swayed about upon a rocking-horse,
And thought it Pegasus,"

we may regret that to make his attack upon these
cavaliers he should have chosen to mount a steed of
the same description, only with the rockers out of
joint. Bulwer Lytton's onslaught on contemporary
verse was perhaps tinged with old-fashioned prejudice,
but the parody in "Kenelm Chillingly" scarcely

exaggerates the distressing effect of this particular form of the modern reaction. On the rare occasion on which Shakespeare seriously and continuously employs the heroic couplet he perhaps instinctively limits the overflow, which it was impossible, in view of effective dramatic expression, altogether to avoid. Anyone may test this by comparing the rhymed with the un-rhymed portions of "Midsummer Night's Dream"; and in the soliloquy of Friar Laurence, at the beginning of the third scene of the second act of " Romeo and Juliet," there is not an instance of *enjambement* in the whole space of thirty lines. These lines, taken sepa-rately, are neither more nor less harmonious than those of the sonnets, or of the prologue to the same act, with which they may easily be compared, nor are the rhymes much better or much worse ; and therefore if their combined effect is less pleasing, we are led to find the reason of this discrepancy in the fabric of the verse itself, which calls for a greater sacrifice of the pregnant sense than the poet was willing to make. Each line of the heroic couplet ends with a challenge, so speedily taken up that we cannot help noticing when the challenge is inadequately met. Thus in—

> " Many for many virtues excellent
> None but for some and yet all different "—

we have a rhyme certainly not more defective than this from the sonnets :

> " Or whether doth my mind, being crowned with you,
> Drink up the monarch's plague, this *flattery*,

Or whether shall I say, mine eye saith true,
And that your love taught it this *alchemy?*"

And yet it is probable that most ears will be more
keenly *conscious* of defect in the first than in the second
instance. But our illustration has a farther bearing.
When Atterbury says, " Mr. Waller brought in more
polysyllables," he means in the body, not the ex-
tremity of the line; the whole tendency of the im-
provement, real or supposed, in this kind is to limit
the use of polysyllables in rhyme, and above all to
banish their concurrence. Here we have a second
enervating influence. A kind of verse thus doubly
restricted, if an impediment to the natural utterance
of thought, is fatal to the effective utterance of passion.
This is in part the account of the brief and long-
forgotten reign of rhymed verse upon the English
stage, as compared with its continuous ascendancy in
the French tragic drama, amid all vicissitudes of taste
and schools, from Corneille to Victor Hugo. We
open Corneille at random, and find abundance of
couplets like this:

"Reste du sang ingrat d'un époux *infidèle*
Héritier d'une flamme envers moi *criminelle.*"

As we find also abundance like this:

"Otez-moi donc de *doute*
Et montrez-moi la main qu'il faut que je *redoute.*"

We have here something more than the licence[1] of
Chaucer and Shakespeare combined; and assuredly

[1] A friend has inferred from this that I suppose such rhymes
to be a licence in *French;* that was not at all my meaning.

no great "bondage" to the poet. But the favourite
line of the days of Dryden and of Pope was a
"bondage"; at once the effect and the cause of a
narrow range of thought. Pope tells us, with admirable satire, of the men who—

> "Ring round the same unvaried chimes,
> With sure returns of still expected rhymes;
> Where'er you find 'the cooling western breeze'
> In the next line, it 'whispers through the trees;'
> If crystal streams 'with pleasing murmurs creep'·
> The reader's threatened (not in vain) with 'sleep.'"

He little suspected that the time was to come when he
himself would be charged with making poetry "a mere
mechanic art." And surely it is not by the novelty of
his rhymes that he delivers us from the sense of the
inevitable and the recurrent; his subtle genius does
not escape these trammels, but only wears them with
a difference. Dryden, as we think, is not in the direct
line of this insensible servitude; the "two coursers"
which Gray bestows upon him are a little restive; and
sometimes give a stimulating shock to his "car." On
other grounds than this it is impossible to class Dryden,
and his wide sympathies and affinities, with the precision which some modern criticism affects. To talk
of "the school of Dryden and Pope" is above all misleading. He who wrote the "Annus Mirabilis" and
the verses on Anne Killigrew grasps Cowley with his
left hand and Milton with his right. He sometimes
passes without hesitation from the province of pure
poetry or the truth of nature to that large domain of

H

"wit," as our ancestors called it, which tempted irre-
sistibly so many ingenious minds. But this temptation
is limited to no age and no school. The much-abused
terms of " classical " and " romantic," in whatever sense
we may employ them, are here an unprofitable distinction.   Is Spenser a romantic poet ?   Addison (but
who now reads Addison ?) tells us that, like Milton,
Spenser has a genius much above that sort of ingenuity
which pushes to extravagance the metaphoric use of
words.   Is Waller a classic poet ?   Addison again
tells us that Mr. Waller—as Ovid also among the Latin
writers—has a great deal of it.   And the truth is that
there is in almost all literature this tendency towards
" conceits," and their fitness must be judged of by a
sense at once finer and healthier than a formal criticism
can bestow. We may agree with Dryden that Ovid's
Dido to Æneas is a poor rival to the fourth Æneid ;
without denying that ingenuity has here some charm.
And it is not criticism, but the experience of life that
must tell us at last whether sad or sick men play
nicely with their names like Ajax or John of Gaunt,
and whether we hear truth to nature or fanciful extravagance when Laertes says—

> " Too much of water has thou, poor Ophelia,
> And therefore I forbid my tears."

And, again, what can Pope himself reply, or we reply
for Pope, to surly Dennis, when he objects that in the
encounter between the ladies and the beaux in the
" Rape of the Lock," " We have a real combat and a

metaphorical dying"? The charge is true: this is an egregious example of metaphor displacing truth, and that after a very dramatic and objective fashion: Addison, nay the "Essay on Criticism" itself, is here set at naught. Dennis is right; but the world is pleased; for Pope is never tedious and does not go beyond the licence which the reader is willing to concede him. And has there ever been a time, since our literature was in any sense vital, when there was not the critical sense, generically the same which Pope and Addison exhibit in a highly developed form, insisting, as they insisted, on sobriety and restraint? Chaucer's "Host of the Tabard" sums up, in very trenchant fashion, the corrective function of criticism when he interrupts "The Rime of Sir Thopas" with

"No more of this for Goddes dignitee."

The same literature supplies the bane and the antidote. The Elizabethan euphuism encounters its satirist in Shakespeare, its critic in Gabriel Harvey, its counterfoil (as well as censor[1]) in Sir Philip Sidney. Later on we find Ben Jonson uttering a timely warning against a new form of extravagance when he advises that "it is fit to read the best authors to youth first, and those the openest and clearest, as Sidney before Donne." And if that "Son of Ben Jonson," George Morley, the future Bishop of Winchester, gave, as we are told, counsels in literature to Waller, we have another evidence that the spiritual succession of good sense was

[1] See "Apologie for Poesie," p. 68, Arber's reprint.

never interrupted, in spite of a transient fashion. Let us concede, though it is a large concession, that in Waller what our forefathers called " wit " predominated over poetry. His merit is that he knew how to manage this faculty ; that he did not, like Cowley, play with figures and semblances, until the thing to be signified was almost lost from sight. To him belongs that chastened sort of fancy, of which we have the perfect flower in the " Rape of the Lock." It is unlikely perhaps that Pope could ever have seen the pretty lines " Upon a Lady's Fishing with an Angle," which we thank Mr. Thorn Drury for printing for the first time ; but when we read—

> " *Each golden hair's a fishing line,*
> Able to catch such hearts as mine,"

who can help thinking of the ever-memorable couplets :

> " With hairy springes we the birds betray,
> Slight lines of hair surprise the finny prey,
> Fair tresses man's imperial race ensnare
> And beauty draws us with a single hair " ?

But here is another parallel, of quite a different *genus* which can hardly be accidental. Gray had certainly read the lines :

> " Great Julius, on the mountain bred,
> A flock perhaps, or herd, had led,
> He that the world subdued had been
> But the best wrestler on the green.
> *'Tis art and knowledge which draw forth*
> The hidden seeds of native worth ;
> They blow those sparks, and make them rise
> Into such flames as touch the skies."

His Hampden, and Cromwell,[1] and Milton, like Waller's Cæsar, perish in obscurity through lack of the "ample page" of knowledge. The thought is exactly the same, but how different the context in which it occurs! Zelinda, "that fairest piece of well-formed earth," whose resolve to wed "none but a prince" is the theme on which Waller blends this serious thought with the praise of her eyes, was probably never anything but the "shadow of a shade"; this is not the setting in which we expect to find those touches which make us realize the pathos of human life. The poets of this generation were too often like the voyagers in Browning's "Paracelsus," who set up their splendid shrines and statues upon a bleak and desolate rock. Waller's powers would certainly be in higher repute, but for the trivial or transitory interests to which he gave them. The court poet pays dearly for his courtliness at last. He bestows the best of his experience upon perishable or unprofitable matter, and we are surprised rather than pleased to find not the fly in amber, but amber in the fly. It was a theory of Waller's, fathered no doubt by his circumstances and his consequent practice, that the poet's sphere was one in which real emotion had no place. " He wrote," he tells us, " with high conceit " when he was free, but—

"Who will describe a storm must not be there.
Passion writes well, neither in love nor fear."

---

[1] From the Mason MS. of the "Elegy" we find that Gray originally wrote "Cæsar" for "Cromwell," as he wrote "Cato" and "Tully" for "Hampden" and "Milton."

His famous answer to Charles II., " Poets, sir, succeed
better in fiction than in truth," was not, we see, altogether an impromptu. We may smile at Johnson's
scorn of Waller's frivolous topics ; we may attribute it
to the fact that *he* was, above all, a moralist ; but his
censure marks also the clearer conviction of a generation for whom the age of patronage had happily passed
away, that poetry if it is to last long must be deeply
rooted in real feeling ; must have, if not serious, at
least adequate aims.

Want of sincere feeling is the secret of Waller's
principal defect, the discrepancy between the separate
parts of each poem, so that very few of them form a
perfect whole, and those such as " Go, lovely Rose," or
the verses " On a Girdle," among the shortest. For
sincerity, though by no means a guarantee for a sustained level of achievement, is at least a great stimulus
in this direction. Cowley's perverse ingenuity is most
conspicuous where he has set himself, with no real
passion, to write his " Mistress " as a fashionable task ;
and he gets rid of almost all his extravagance in his
" Elegy on the Death of William Hervey," and of
much of it in those original verses, the fruit of genuine
experience, which he inserts in his Essays. Analog-
ously, we believe that if Waller's themes had been
chosen by him with more spontaneity, and in a more
independent spirit, we should find fewer instances in
his pages of incongruity and bathos. As it is, some of
his best lines have all the appearance of "ideas for
verses " kept in reserve for any " copy " to which they

might be made to fit. We have quoted, in our first example of Waller's manner, the most serious thought of his life, both in its earliest and in its latest form. But in that earliest form it is linked with a trumpery pagan simile so utterly out of keeping that it is a sin even to quote it in such a connection. Poets who work after a different fashion suffer when we pluck choice passages from the context, and serve them up as elegant extracts ; in Waller's case, this is often the best service we can render his fame. For instance, take these lines " On the Picture of a Fair Youth after he was Dead " :

> " As gathered flowers, while their wounds are new,
> Look gay and fresh, as on the stalk they grew :
> Torn from the root that nourished them, awhile
> (Not taking notice of their fate) they smile,
> And in the hand which rudely plucked them, show
> Fairer than those that to their autumn grow ;
> So love and beauty still that visage grace ;
> Death cannot fright them from their wonted place.
> Alive the hand of cruel Age had marred
> Those lovely features, which cold Death has spared."

This is very beautiful; but we have stopped in time, just before Waller tells us that it was no wonder that the young man " sped in love so well " when he had breath to tell "his high passion," and no other business than " to persuade that dame " whose mutual love advanced him so high that heaven was but the next step. And the truth is that we have but quoted one of Waller's cherished images ; he has used it, with but a slight variation adapted to the circumstances, in

his address, *À la Malade*, the lovely Amoret, whom
heaven " solicits," he says—

> " With such a care
> As roses from their stalks we tear,
> When we would still preserve them new
> And fresh, as on the bush they grew."

Again, Waller never wrote prettier verses than the
opening lines in the poem " Of the Queen " :

> " The lark that shuns on lofty boughs to build
> Her humble nest, lies silent in the field;
> But if the promise of a cloudless day,
> Aurora smiling, bids her rise and play,
> Then straight she shows 'twas not for want of voice,
> Or power to climb, she made so low a choice;
> Singing she mounts; her airy wings are stretched
> Towards heaven, as if from heaven her note she fetched."

But if we would remain pleased we must not read
much farther. We are in the descending scale. Her
Majesty's admirers are weaned from all meaner affections ; they are like a traveller who has mistaken the
glow-worm for a diamond, and " casts the worthless
worm away " when better informed by the sunshine ;
royalty, hitherto in the character of Aurora, next becomes a surgeon :

> " She saves the lover, as we gangrenes stay,
> By cutting hope, like a lopped limb away,
> This makes her bleeding patients to accuse
> High Heaven "—

and the reader to accuse something else. We have
attributed to Waller a certain measure of that good

sense which is indispensable to any poetry which is to
be read from generation to generation; but these
instances are enough to show us how partial in him
the triumph of good sense was; once started on a
simile, he knows, better than most of his contemporaries, when to stop; he is scarcely better in-
structed than the poets of the so-called metaphysical
school when not to begin. He makes no endeavour
after that uniformity of tone, which in all great poets
is an instinct, and in many minor poets a conscious
aim. That maxim, " Survey the whole," which Pope
pleads in arrest of judgment on particular blemishes,
is equally valid as a preventive; we recognize better
what was the really solid service rendered to our
literature by that epoch which he and Addison interpret for us, when we see poems so finished and
graceful in some respects as Waller's subject to such
collapses of structure. Waller knew the *word* " bathos"
and its meaning; he knew the opening lines of the
" Ars Poetica," and all about the "*purpureus pannus*,"
yet often enough in a set of his verses the "*purpureus
pannus*" is the one noteworthy thing. What is more,
to Dryden also and to Atterbury the " Ars Poetica "
was a kind of Decalogue; yet they do but praise
Waller for his choice of words and ease of numbers,
and betray (so far as we are aware) no suspicion of
the radical defect which we have noted. Atterbury is
content to look back upon the reign of Charles II. as
the Augustan age of English; and Waller himself, with
his characteristic economy of thought, and not, we may

be sure, without some notion of his own contribution
to the desired result, twice tells us that—

"Our lines reformed, and not composed in haste,
Polished like marble, would like marble last."

The words of Persius:

"Quis populi sermo est?   Quis enim? nisi carmina molli
Nunc demum numero fluere, ut per leve severos
Effundat iunctura ungues"—

exactly express the measure of success which Waller
aimed at achieving and his admirers thought he had
achieved, neither the artist nor his judges supposing
that much remained to do, and that something more
is necessary for sculpture than the material and the
polish.

The office of the professional mourner or panegyrist
lends itself too readily to bathos, which is often only
the transition from utterances which, however applied,
were once conceived in real feeling, to taskwork exe-
cuted in a more frigid mood.   Waller had a genuine
sense of beauty, and especially of Nature's loveliness
in little things; in this respect he has something of
Herrick's bias; something also, in treating such objects,
of Herrick's skill.   But he very often makes us think
of a miniature-painter who has set to work upon too
large a canvas, and displaying only on a part of it his
special aptitude, fills in the rest with some coarser and
cheaper kind of dexterity, which he has also at command.   Waller has touches of real tenderness—at least,
so they impress us.   When creatures young and

beautiful perish, or are ready to perish, he seems possessed with genuine pity for their fate; a nature essentially kindly, combined assuredly with experience, to write for " the tomb of the only son of the Lord Andover " the lines :

> " Like buds appearing ere the frosts are passed, ·
> To become man he made such fatal haste,
> And to perfection laboured so to climb,
> Preventing slow experience and time,
> That 'tis no wonder Death our hopes beguiled,
> He's seldom old that will not be a child."

We should be sorry to think that here he is advantaged by that " fiction " which he professed to think necessary to poetic success. Here as elsewhere Waller's thought is epigrammatic ; but epigram does not exclude pathos. Perhaps fancy was never more touchingly employed than in those lines of Martial on the youthful charioteer, whose thread, he says, Lachesis cut, because, counting his palms of victory, she mistook him for an old man. Such a thought would have been welcomed by Waller, who deplores in very kindred strains—

> " The learned Savile's heir,
> So early wise, and lasting fair,
> That none except her years they told
> Thought her a child, or thought her old."

The present generation, with its rather Pharisaic discourse about "high seriousness " in the matter of poetry, needs to be reminded that wit, in its old-fashioned sense, had once a larger province than we

are disposed to give it ; that it could be graceful in
tears as in laughter ; and bore its part in interpreting
the severer aspects of man's destiny.   In one of those
pleasant oases with which Porson skilfully relieved
the monotony of textual criticism he reminds us that
the figure of the eagle slain by an arrow winged with
his own feathers (with which Waller, after *his* manner
addresses a lady "singing a song of his composing ")
was anticipated by the sombre muse of Æschylus.
We will not then blame Waller for devoting his
characteristic gift to elegy; nor would this use of it
even *seem* false in tone, but that it is employed on the
same occasion to pay an incongruous tribute to the
living.   He is at his best and at his worst in compliment ; at his best because no one can turn a compliment more gracefully ; at his worst because he
never knows when a compliment is out of place altogether.   We are dangerously near to the disgust which
on certain themes pretty *make-believes* always inspire,
when, addressing " the Lord Admiral, on his late sickness and recovery," he says of the brother and sister
of the convalescent that—

> "As lilies overcharged with rain, they bend
> Their beauteous heads, and with high heaven contend,
> *Fold thee within their snowy arms*, and cry—
> ' He is too faultless, and too young, to die ! ' "

Let us repeat that *bathos* was at this time an
epidemic for which the preventive, if known, was
neglected.   This will help us to understand why
Waller, who can write of the Lady Rich—

> "Some happy angel, that beholds her there,
> Instruct us to record what she was here!"—

can also write in the same context—

> "That horrid word, at once like lightning spread,
> Struck all our ears—The Lady Rich is dead!"

From this to the couplet from an unsuccessful prize poem on the "Recovery of the Prince of Wales"—

> "Hour after hour the electric message came,
> 'He is not better; but is much the same'"—

is surely but a step. Pope has a great tenderness for Waller, yet he cannot help including in "Martinus Scriblerus on the Bathos" the example—

> "Under the tropics is our language spoke
> And part of Flanders has received our yoke."

But a less friendly critic might have cited many another instance. In the absence of critical warnings, there was one pitfall, into which Dryden, as well as Waller, sometimes tumbles, in the custom of treating contemporary events historically in verse. In the Duke of York's sea-fight with Opdam, the Earl of Falmouth, Lord Muskerry, and Mr. Boyle were killed at the Duke's side by a volley; this was a fact too important to be omitted, and so Waller writes—

> "Three worthy persons from his side it tore,
> And dyed his garment with their scattered gore."

Much as, according to Macaulay, one of the many poetasters on the Battle of Blenheim invites us to—

"Think of two thousand gentlemen at least,
And each man mounted on his capering beast;
Into the Danube they were pushed by shoals."

Even Addison's " Campaign " is by no means free
from this blemish, though, if we would judge of this,
we must read not the instances given with apologetic
malice in Pope's " Martinus Scriblerus," but the specimen over which Dick Steele, with a tenderness inspired by wine and friendship, hiccups in a certain
chapter of " Esmond."

When Aubrey tells us of those courtiers who made
Waller tipsy at Somerset House so that " at the water-
stayres he fell downe, and had a cruel fall," he adds
that, " 'Twas pitty to use such a sweet swan so in-
humanely." Something of the same compunction ought
to be felt by the critic when he anatomizes in cold
blood this sweet swan's cygnets.   When much has
been said about him in the seventeenth century and
something in the nineteenth which savours of exaggeration, it is useful to try to fix his real place and merit.
We have seen that we must not attribute to him a
great importance in the history of English metre ;
even in the heroic couplet which he undoubtedly
helped to popularize, he did not, as Johnson remarks,
dispense with expletives ; and in such lines as

　　　" *At once* they promise what *at once* they give,"
and
　　　" *Resolved* to conquer, or *resolved* to die,"

we have feeble efforts after that antithetic manner in
which a later generation achieved a not very valuable

success. It is far more serviceable to realize what he
was in the substance of his verse and the character of
his thoughts. We cannot difference him from his
contemporaries in the terms of any school. Like the
metaphysical poets he abounds in hyperbole, conceits,
far-fetched resemblances ; his distinctive mark is that
in the use of these he is more dexterous, more finished,
restrained, concise. You cannot go much further than
to say, that only while the hand of sleep closes the
eyes of royalty can the sun boast itself " the brightest
thing that shines " ; but having uttered his daring
paradox Waller is contented to have done with it.
To connect Westminster Abbey with the summit of a
volcano was a hazardous experiment such as Cowley
would have delighted to make. Waller *has* made it ;
the House of Parliament where " all our ills were
shaped " stood hard by ; yet the temple was un-
harmed :

> " So snow on Ætna does unmelted lie,
> Whence rolling flames and scattered cinders fly ;
> The distant country in the ruin shares ;
> What falls from heaven the burning mountain spares."

There is a certain art here employed to disguise
from us the remoteness of the analogy ; we feel that
at the same date almost any other of our minor poets,
if the same fancy struck him, would have laboured to
excite our wonder how any mortal man could have
thought of such a resemblance at all. Again, Waller
is an accomplished man ; an Etonian and a King's
man, he is an elegant Latin verse-writer, though when

we remember that in his rendering of one of his own
English poems, skilful as it is, he makes the substan-
tive "laurea" a neuter plural, we cannot call him
exact; and, like the metaphysical poets, he makes
great use of whatever learning he possesses for the
purpose of his song.   In particular he deals, like them,
with notions of science; but with a truer, because a
more sober, ingenuity than theirs.   The accident that
he knew less than they combines with a better instinc-
tive taste than theirs to make him give us such lines
as these " To the Mutable Fair " :

> "The formal stars do travel so
> As we their names and courses know,
> And he that on their changes looks
> Would think them governed by our books;
> But never were the clouds reduced
> To any art; the motions used
> By those free vapours are so light,
> So frequent, that the conquered sight
> Despairs to find the rules that guide
> Those gilded shadows as they slide."

And though Johnson affirms that he is there " too
much of a Copernican," what strikes us yet more is
the finished adroitness, with which in praise of " De
Mornay's eyes " he tells the sun—

> "Well does this prove
> The error of those antique books,
> Which made you move
> About the world; her charming looks
> Would fix your beams, and make it ever day,
> Did not the rolling earth snatch her away."

In fact there is an air of simplicity about Waller's boldest strokes; he delivers them as if they were the most natural things in the world. He is, perhaps, as ambitious as any other of his day to display whatever erudition he possesses; happy therefore in his comparative ignorance; for learning in his time encumbered the wings of poetry; and there was only one song-bird, and that song-bird Milton, whom it helped to fly.

There is one praise of Waller which no critic should omit, for, considering the nature of so many of his themes and the age in which he wrote, it is specially honourable to him, and throws the best and latest aspect of his character into high relief. If in the volume before us we have all that he ever wrote it must be acknowledged that, though often trivial, he is singularly free from vicious suggestions, and that in the old man's regrets for his wasted powers we are to read nothing more than a wish that he had given them to those religious meditations which are the subject of his last poems, and of his longest, that " Of the Divine Love." His literary reputation has suffered from association with less respectable names, from certain strange and almost inexplicable episodes in his political career, and from the impression, thence in part derived, that he was a man of defective moral sense. In the reaction towards a purer tone in letters which Steele and Addison helped to bring about, his fame as a writer suffered from that injustice which, according to Macaulay, the British public, in its periodic fits of morality, always inflicts; and the innocent "Verses on a Girdle" were actually selected for censure. The history of the plot which goes by his name shows that he proved weak and ignoble under the fear of death ; that he was dissolute when he was for a while a widower has been affirmed of him, and is possibly true ; but he was an affectionate husband and father, and there is evidence that in his latter years the man was much respected and even beloved. If in turning his mercurial pages we do not expect to find any sense of the seriousness of life, let it be to his credit that it is there; that even *there* "are tears for sad events and the estate of mortal men touches the soul." A transcript of the lines entitled "Of the last Verses in the Book" is headed "The last verses my dear ffather made," and let this little domestic tribute be for us as a volume of forgotten praise in a region to which history and criticism have no access, while we copy, for their unmistakable note of sincerity, the words to which Waller's title refers ;—

"Wrestling with death, these lines I did indite:
No other theme could give my soul delight.
O that my youth had thus employed my pen !
Or that I now could write as I wrote then !
But 'tis of grace, if sickness, age, and pain
Are felt as throes, when we are born again ;
Timely they come to wean us from this earth,
As pangs that wait upon a second birth."

JOHN GAY

I F Gay were living now, what, considering his powers and the character of his gift, would be his place among men of letters? We have some *data* for a comparison, at least in one department; for that light and airy creation, the English comic opera, of which he gave the earliest example, is once more in fashion. The immortality of the *di minorum gentium* of literature is often less the result of genius than of a fortunate choice of theme. In this respect Gay has been more than usually happy. He is the prototype of a class of writers still in vogue; he is the describer also of scenes and manners and customs which still have no remote interest for all Englishmen. Again, like La Fontaine and (if we may be pardoned an association so incongruous in other respects) Dr. Watts, Gay has conquered by stooping; and the author of "The Hare with Many Friends" lives with the historian of " Le Lion et le Moucheron " and the panegyrist of the little "Busy Bee."

The present age would perhaps rank Gay lowest in that kind of writing in which, in his own time, he achieved a phenomenal success. The " Beggar's

Opera" is very coarse homespun compared with the
dainty fabrics which have come from the loom of
Mr. W. S. Gilbert.   Both artists have the merit of
a naïve simplicity ; but we are on a lower plane of wit
and humour altogether when we pass from the delicate
satire of

> "When everybody's somebody
> Nobody's anybody"—

to—

> "Since laws were made for every degree
> To curb vice in others, as well as in me,
> I wonder we ha'nt better company
>   Upon Tyburn tree."

Or—

> " How happy could I be with either,
>   Were t'other dear charmer away;
> But while you thus tease me together,
>   To neither a word will I say
>   But tol de rol," etc.

These strains, so captivating to Dukes and
Duchesses in 1728, are better suited, for a continuance,
to the taste of Tony Lumpkin's friends, or of the
lustige Gesellen in Auerbach's cellar. Of the "Splendid
Shilling" of John Philips Johnson has said, with much
truth, that "the merit of such performances begins and
ends with the first author." He might have said the
same of the "Beggar's Opera" considered as an
attempt to set Newgate on Parnassus.

Yet in one respect the songs of the "Beggar's
Opera," of "Polly," and of the "What-d'ye Call It?"
have a certain interest for the critic. They are an
early symptom of a desire for a little more ease in

eighteenth-century verse. Not by any means a serious
reaction ; the stately heroics or Alexandrines were no
more to be discarded than wigs and shoe-buckles.
The lyrist himself sometimes seems tickled with a
sense of his own absurdity; and we think of a company
of highly dressed personages enjoying a game of Puss-
in-the-Corner, or Blind Man's Buff. The story of
Cowper (to Unwin, August 4, 1783), on the joint
authorship of the ballad in the "What-d'ye Call It?"
is questioned by Mr. Underhill, although Cowper
professes to speak on good authority. It is not
difficult of credit, and it is quite in keeping with the
vein in which the thing, as we suppose, was done,
that " the most celebrated association of clever fellows
this country ever saw—Swift, Arbuthnot, Pope, and
Gay—united their strength and abilities in the composition of a song." Only, when Cowper adds that
they " did not think it beneath them," he perhaps
gives the business too serious a *nuance* for the humour
in which we conceive it to have been undertaken.
" Let us lend friend Gay a hand," we can fancy these
greater gods saying, bursting in upon the little fat
poet who is racking his brains in that most painful of
all tasks, the quest of things sprightly or naïve.
Arbuthnot, the satirist with little acrimony, and Swift,
the satirist with much, were both, we may be sure,
letting their wits take a holiday on this occasion.
Pope too, the youngest and the most malicious
member of this strange confederacy, must certainly
have enjoyed this opportunity of indirectly mocking

the pastoral simplicity of Ambrose Philips once more. Is it possible to conceive such a *junto* capping verses over a love-sick maiden without banter? We rather picture them rolling in their chairs to the sing-song measure as each contributes his couplet or quatrain :

> "The merchant robb'd of pleasure
> Sees tempests in despair;
> But what's the loss of treasure
> To the losing of my dear?
> Should you some coast be laid on
> Where gold and di'monds grow,
> You'll find a richer maiden,
> But none that loves you so."

Gay alone here was pursuing something like his proper trade ; but for the rest, *if* they had a hand in it, it was with the unextinguishable laughter proper to such an Olympus.

We a little incline to believe Cowper's tradition, because this particular ballad has a quite extraordinary character of simplicity, which, successful as it is, savours of a jest. It may, of course, be altogether by the same hand that wrote "Sweet William's Farewell to Black-eyed Susan." The first half of the century, as Cowper says, was rich in kindred productions, a fact quite compatible with the other fact, that they were not undertaken with much " high seriousness." The poet " buckled to " his epic, which men have forgotten, but he "threw off" his ballad, which they remember. Who now knows anything of Glover's Leonidas? But, at least for historians and note-makers, "Hosier's Ghost"

still walks. So does " Margaret's Ghost," whom Mallet
raised again ; and she takes her revenge now upon the
faithless sex by betraying schoolboys into false quan-
tities in their attempts to translate her into Latin
elegiacs. Mallet's " Amyntor and Theodora," to whom
he gave epic dignity and so many blank verses, are
the real ghosts now; the merest shadow of a shade.
Tickell's monody on the death of Addison is praised,
but, with the exception of two lines, scarcely remembered ; but his " Lucy and Colin " may continue
for some time yet to draw tears, perhaps not very
sentimental, in the classroom. Cowper, with a judgment pleasantly coloured by affection, affirms that
Vincent Bourne's renderings of these ballads of Tickell
and Gay and Mallet are more beautiful than the
originals, and surpass all that Ovid and Tibullus have
left behind them. Discounting as much as we please
from this opinion, we shall always have the *residuum*
that these things are translatable because they deal
with the emotions which are always with us, on the
safe plane of common—that is to say, universal, sense.

Let us not forget that Addison, with that insight
into first principles which is the critic's "harvest of
the quiet eye," had, as early as 1711, in two papers
upon "Chevy Chase," noted that the secret of the
vitality and power of the songs of the people lies in
their truth to the permanent elements of human nature.
He exhumes Sidney's acknowledgment that the old
song of Percy and Douglas, though sung but " by some
blind crowder," " moved his heart more than with a

trumpet"; and he dissents from Sidney's judgment
on "the rude style and evil apparel" of the song, etc.[1]
Sidney is here, perhaps, hampered by those academic
prejudices which expect literature to be ornate.   His
own practice was not extravagant; but the euphuism
of his generation and its various developments were
bound to end in the conceits of the metaphysical poets
and a fashion of self-conscious, ambitious, elaborate
effort.   Addison's retrospect is upon a literature which,
sharing as he did the dominant taste in architecture,
he calls, by way of disparagement, Gothic; and he
sets himself, in defiance of ridicule, to prove an epic
dignity, the majestic simplicity of a Parthenon, in
"Chevy Chase."   But it may be doubted whether the
result of these endeavours to recommend "nature"
was at all commensurate with their courage.   The
simplicity of the ballad was a relief, but it was not
business; there was, perhaps, throughout the eighteenth
century a feeling, latent rather than expressed, that
anything great and serious must be announced with a
certain pomp of manner.   We see traces of this in
Johnson's "Lives of the Poets."   What is written
with directness and without obvious pains, especially
if it lacks a definite moral, he is disposed to slur; he
thinks of all such verses what he *says* of Swift's, that
"they offer little upon which the critic can exercise

[1] Addison did not know, what Percy made clear, that the
ballad, in the form in which *he* knew it, was a later version.
The "Chevy Chase" which Sidney had heard is the first of the
"Reliques."

his powers." Indeed, after the publication of the "Reliques" he had sniffed the coming breeze, and snorted with a derision which found vent *extempore* in parody—

> "As with my hat upon my head
> I walked into the Strand,
> I there did meet another man
> With *his* hat in his hand."[1]

Yet undoubtedly, as far as Gay survives, he owes his vitality in part to the modesty of aim, the apparent directness, pleasing still, because not spoiled by obsolete affectations, which is found in some of his songs, and which helps to make so much of ballad poetry immortal. In his heroics Gay is unsuccessful just as far as he is ambitious. Whatever pleasure these gave to his own generation was the pleasure men find in seeing *trivial* things (the word is oddly in place here) versified. The lady who, as he tells us, advised him—

> "No more let trifling themes your muse employ
> Nor lavish verse to paint a female toy,"

was no wise monitress. The "female toy" is the "Fan," and Gay's "Fan," if not a success, enables us at least to fix the limits of his imaginative powers. It scarcely conveys the right impression to say, with Mr. Austin Dobson, that it is "unreadable"; it is the

---

[1] On another occasion, when he thought he could beat Percy's version of "Rio verde," etc., he betrays his epoch completely—"*Confused in mutual slaughter*" is part of *his* rendering.

second and third books that betray the inexhaustible
spinner of conventional verse. The first should have
an interest for us, because in it (perhaps even in the
others to some extent) are resemblances to the "Rape
of the Lock," and it seems at first sight to the credit
of Pope, and an evidence of the engaging character of
Gay, that the "Fan" excited the interest instead of
the jealousy of the poet, whose malice was on the alert
against rivals so little formidable as Ambrose Philips
and Tickell. Let us quote from Gay's description of
the work of the Cupids, published on the 8th of
December, 1713 :

> "A different toil another forge employs;
> Here the loud hammer fashions female toys,
> Hence is the fair with ornaments supplied,
> Hence sprung the glittering implements of pride;
> Each trinket that adorns the modern dame
> First to these little artists owed its frame.
> Here an unfinish'd *di'mond crosslet lay*,
> *To which soft lovers adoration pay;*
> There was the polish'd crystal bottle seen,
> That with quick scents revives the modish spleen;
> Here the yet rude unjointed snuff-box lies,
> *Which serves the rallied fop for smart replies;*
> There piles of paper rose in gilded reams,
> The future records of the lover's flames;
> Here clouded canes 'midst heaps of toys are found,
> And inlaid tweezer cases strew the ground.
> There stands the Toilette, nursery of charms,
> Completely furnish'd with bright beauty's arms;
> The patch, the powder-box, pulville, perfumes,
> Pins, paint, a flatt'ring glass, and black lead combs."

Who can help thinking of Belinda's toilet here?

But the superior artist first published those new touches to his delightful poem on March 2, 1714. On the other hand, Gay's "diamond crosslet"—

"To which softs lovers adoration pay,"

The "clouded canes"; and the snuff-box—

"Which serves the rallied fop for smart replies;"

are feeble *reminiscences* of that cross, which in 1712 Belinda already—

"wore
Which Jews might kiss and infidels adore;"

and of the armoury with which Sir Plume was furnished, the "clouded cane" which he nicely "conducted" and the box which he rapped to emphasize his demand for the restoration of the hair. It is not often that literature offers us examples of two poems so coincident in date and cognate in theme, which so well exemplify the difference between genius and mere dexterity. The two friends must have been cognisant each of the other's work; but there could be no rivalry between them. The same materials in the hands of the one receive life and movement, point and grace; in the hands of the other, they are little more than an amusing inventory. But let us not deal too unkindly with Gay, because he thus serves, as Pope no doubt foresaw, as a *foil*. The whole work is indeed overladen with classic and other lumber, and "paintings" of "the enamelled green." But if it had ended with the first book, we should perhaps have been contented to say of it that it was on the whole a pretty little poem, and that, in the phrase of old-fashioned criticism, the invention of the fan from the tail of Juno's peacock was natural and probable. Yet we should judge, after Johnson, who discusses part of this great question as it appears in " Trivia " with due impressiveness, that this kind of invention was not Gay's *forte*. A modern reader dismisses such matters in more summary fashion ; and is satisfied with finding the history of the " patten " mildly entertaining, and the origin of the shoeblack disgusting. The main interest of " Trivia " was always in its realities ; men of that day, as of all days, delighted to read the life they knew well described with some appearance of art. The mere photography of prose needed to be coloured with malice and *innuendo*, as in Swift's " Polite Conversation " or " Directions to Servants." For Gay the pomp of verse and occasional similes served the same purpose of amusing. There was a great and acknowledged resemblance between Swift and Gay in these " touches of things common "; we can scarcely add " till they rose to touch the spheres." Swift had anticipated Gay in " Morning " and in the " City Shower," selecting—after his fashion—London life at its dirtiest moment. The misanthrope and the man of " mild affections " had both of them the eye of a Dutch painter, the humour and the coarseness of the Dutch caricaturist ; and Swift liked to suggest congenial subjects to his " brother of the brush." But there is a great part of " Trivia " which, divested of its mock heroic tone,

would pass simply for useful information ; we can conceive the country squire making it his text-book in the
prospect of a visit to London ; the comic notion of an
index, which Gay had already adopted in " The
Shepherd's Week," may in " Trivia " have served a
purpose not altogether burlesque.   What directions
are more useful than those which tell men where to
get the best food ?   On the other hand, what simpler
than to say, " Buy your mutton in Newgate Market,
your beef in Leadenhall, your veal in St. James," etc. ?
But the utility of such counsels is not impaired in the
form :

> " Shall the large mutton smoke upon your boards?
> Such Newgate's copious market best affords.
> Would'st thou with mighty beef augment thy meal?
> Seek Leaden-hall ; St. James's sends thee veal ;
> Thames-street gives cheeses ; Covent-garden fruits ;
> Moor-fields old books ; and Monmouth-street old suits.
> Hence may'st thou well supply the wants of life,
> Support thy family, and clothe thy wife."

A curious feature of " Trivia " on this practical side
of it is its minute particularity in the article of clothing.
One cannot help thinking of Gay's apprenticeship to
a silk-mercer : " How long he continued behind the
counter," says Johnson, " or with what degree of soft-
ness and dexterity he received and accommodated the
ladies, as he probably took no delight in telling it,
cannot be known."   But his occupation left its traces
both in his person and in his pen.   At the close of
1713 he is banteringly described by Pope to Swift as,

"An unhappy youth, who writes pastorals during the time of divine service; whose case is the more deplorable, as he hath miserably lavished away all that silver he should have reserved for his soul's health on buttons and hoops for his coat." Surely the origin of this spruceness is not far to seek. And the wear suitable for every season is described in "Trivia" with an exactitude which we could scarcely find except among experts. Thus of coats in winter he writes:

> "Now in thy trunk thy D'oily habit fold,
> The silken drugget ill can fence the cold;
> The frieze's spongy nap is soak'd with rain,
> And showers soon drench the camlet's cockled grain,
> True Witney broadcloth with its shag unshorn,
> Unpierced is in the lasting tempest worn."

Indeed, this learning proved too profound for the general reader, and in a note to a later edition Gay explains that Witney is a town in Oxfordshire. With the same precision he describes the risks of soiling which vary with the attire; he who wears the "reverend gown" must beware especially of contact with the barber, the perfumer, and the baker; those who walk in "youthful colours" must avoid the chimney-sweep, the small-coal-man, the dustman, the chandler, and the butcher.[1] The fop and the miller are also a danger,

---

[1] We are reminded of poor Kit Smart's wonderful simile:

> "Thus when a barber and a collier fight
> The barber beats the luckless collier *white;*
> The dusty collier heaves his ponderous sack,
> And big with vengeance, beats the barber *black;*

for from both a powder, though of different sorts, is apt to fly. A certain side of the business life of London is known to him after an intimate and peculiar fashion ; under his guidance we enter the linen-draper's in wintry weather, and find the shop ladies keeping themselves warm with battledore and shuttlecock *from* counter to counter, while the needles lie useless in the half-whipt muslin ; and passing out, we go into Covent-garden, where the glaziers and truant 'prentices and a motley crowd are playing football with such vigour that we look about us for shelter.

We get from " Trivia " the impression of a street-life rougher, scarcely less noisy, but more leisurely, than the street-life now. We feel that almost all the perils of the *day* in the London of 1716 might have been avoided by a few civil conventions and the most rudi-mentary police. But government was not paternal in those times, and educated its public only as old Mr. Weller educated Sam. Even correction was boisterous, and Gay, always solicitous for the outward man, advises you to give the pillory a wide berth, lest the turnips and addled eggs designed for the " perjured head " should salute your own. Man, the unit, was all in all in encountering these perils ; when the bully cocked his hat as you approached him, it was for your firmness and resolution to decide whether he or you went into

---

In comes the brick-dust man, with grime o'erspread,
And beats the collier and the barber *red;*
Black, red and white in various clouds are tossed,
And in the dust they raise the combatants are lost."

the muddy kennel. The post, fitting counterpart in the London of the eighteenth century to the long rows of Hermes busts in an Athenian street in the days of Pericles, or the tall lamp-posts of to-day, was at once your danger and your safeguard ; if you were heedless in your walk or impertinently curious you were sure to run against it ; but it was the only, though very insufficient, barrier between you and chariots, waggons, and sedan-chairs. These last often intruded ; for the chairmen were, it is well known, a burly and aggressive generation ; supported by the insolent footmen who escorted with torches the great dame to midnight assemblies, they trespassed within the limits with impunity ; and the poet often knocked his knees against the poles of chairs left standing at the doors. But sometimes, as in the pass of St. Clement Danes, the pedestrian found himself—

"Where not a post protects the narrow space,"

and pushed his way stooping under the low penthouses, whilst beside him waggoners slashed at each other from their high seats, or fought with fists afoot ; and blaspheming drovers urged the frightened cattle through the press. With a little more intensity and purpose Gay might be called the Hogarth of the pen ; he leaves on you the same impression of squalor and insufficient light. The rails in the squares are lined with rows of whining beggars ; but the man who stops to listen to a piteous plaint at night is likely to be felled to the ground by the crutch which has moved his compassion. The link-boys were often in league

with these dissemblers, and helped them to rifle your
pockets after extinguishing the light. Queer forms of
theft were in vogue, especially at nightfall. If you
turned into a crowd your sword was apt to be stolen
from its scabbard, or your wig removed from your
head by a boy carried in a basket. A worse terror
were the Mohawks, whose prototypes the old blind
indignant bard of " Paradise Lost " had in mind, in his
darkness and solitude when he wrote of—

> "luxurious cities, where the noise
> Of riot ascends above their loftiest towers
> And injury and outrage, and when night
> Darkens the streets, then wander forth the sons
> Of Belial, flown with insolence and wine."

These Mohawks, of whom Swift wrote to Archbishop
King in 1712 that they were " still very troublesome,
and every night cut somebody or other over the face,
and commit a hundred insolent barbarities," were " still
very troublesome " in 1716 ; the more innocent
" Nicker " was still breaking windows with half-pence.
To remedy these mischiefs watchmen shook their
lanterns, and gathered at this signal for a promiscuous
running-in, from which it was possible to escape by
feeing the palm.

> " Happy Augusta ! law-defended town,"

exclaims Gay, without the slightest touch of irony.
He counted himself blessed because he was not liable
to be stabbed, and because London churches gave no
sanctuary to murderers. Perhaps this comfortable
optimism, this complete absence of the " divine discon-

K

tent," may help to account for the fact that, for so
many years afterwards, the capital was still suffering
from the spasmodic energy of its guardians, evils worse
than the good-natured supineness of Dogberry and
Verges.   In 1742, as Horace Walpole tells us, it was
given to these gentlemen to anticipate in London the
horrors of the Black Hole of Calcutta.   They swept,
without distinction, six-and-twenty women of the
poorer classes into St. Martin's Roundhouse.   "One
poor wretch said that she was worth eighteen-pence,
and would gladly give it for a glass of water, but in
vain !"   Six victims died of suffocation, one a poor
creature who was returning home late from washing :
"The same men, on the same night, took up Jack
Spencer, Mr. Stewart, and Lord George Graham, and
would have thrust them into the roundhouse with the
poor women if they had not been worth more than
eighteen-pence !"

We must compare Horace with Juvenal, or Gay's
"Trivia" with Johnson's "London," if we would realize
how diverse are the moods that are called up by the
same scenes, the same bricks and mortar.   Johnson's
imitation is more than an ingenious exercise to turn a
penny; in his "injured Thales" the indignation of
Umbricius after many centuries flames up anew.   Yet,
strange as it seems, as we look at that famous third
satire once more, it is Gay rather than Johnson that
we ask to supply us with the external counterpart to
the life of old Rome ; the chariots rattling past each
other in the narrow street ; the herds brought to a

standstill, whilst the drovers shout and curse ; the civic magnate in his palanquin speeding to pay early court to the wealthy ; even the huge waggon groaning beneath the weight of the quivering pine is balanced in Gay's picture, though the dapper Londoner has no tragic climax to the overturning of *his* ponderous beam, no middle-class Hector crushed beneath it and forgotten, whilst the unsuspecting household is preparing for his return. Perhaps neither "London" nor "Trivia" will ever be *much* read any more ; yet "Trivia" has the better chance, for human indignation does not burn like fire for ever, but curiosity is an enduring passion. Gay is the more likely to profit by that irony of literary history which gives men significance through their very lack of earnest purpose. Time, an ally not subject to casualties, works with those who are content to describe things as they are, and show us the men of their own generation "in their habits as they lived" ; the stars in their courses fight a battle for their fame ; in the retrospect of posterity an imagination more potent than theirs make ghosts grow vivid in proportion as bodies crumble into dust.

Gay's imagination worked slowly, as he found when he set himself to invent fables. "How comes friend Gay to be so tedious?" (meaning dilatory) writes Swift to Pope. "Another man can publish fifty thousand lies sooner than he can publish fifty *fables*." We are assured that these fables are Gay's sole title to the position which he has held among English writers for a century and a half; he is then, one among many

instances of the immortality achieved by pleasing the
simplest minds ; the immortality of Bunyan and Defoe,
of La Fontaine and La Motte Fouqué ; the real as distinguished from the literary or esoteric immortality
even of Swift.   And yet, as Mr. Austin Dobson and
Mr. Underhill remind us, Gay's fables are not exactly
masterpieces.   One naturally compares him with La
Fontaine, but the comparison at once suggests a very
essential difference.   For La Fontaine really seems to
live the life of his creatures, and to give them just the
articulate speech which, if they could, they would use.
" By Jove," says an impertinent squireen, in one of
Trollope's novels, to the Irish parson who has been
describing with unerring precision the course which
the fox *must* have taken, and the motives which *must*
have guided him, " I believe you were once a fox
yourself."   To fit the same theory of transmigration to
La Fontaine we should have to suppose that he was
once the whole animal kingdom.   Of this versatility
Gay has no trace.[1]   Read the fable of " The Degenerate Bees," for instance, and vexed at a silly

---

[1] We must except his monkeys.   They are not so happily
imagined as the monkeys in the " Jungle Books," but their conceit is well rendered :

> " how fantastic is the sight
> To meet men always bolt upright,
> Because we sometimes walk on two !
> I hate the imitating crew ! "

But the power to give characteristic speech to the animal world
was not largely bestowed in the interval between La Fontaine
and Rudyard Kipling.

disguise which amounts to nothing more than the mention of a hive and some cells, you will ask angrily, " Why *bees ?* " There is really more of personation in Gay's " Pins and Needles " than in his living things. The main purpose of his *menagerie* is to depreciate man ; and a curious and systematic reader, who should take Gay seriously, would discover that the only animal upon whom man can look down from a higher moral elevation is—of all creatures in the world—the turkey. Gay belongs to a fashionable school, in which there was but one sincere professor ; and even the terrible earnestness of Swift was as powerless as the affectation of the rest to disturb the latent satisfaction of humanity. Most of those extremely comfortable people, who placed their own species in the most un-favourable contrast with the brute creation, would have opened their eyes wide could they have lived into the generation which at the close of the century did its utmost to make their meaning good. The monotonous abundance of these opinions was an evidence how lightly they were held ; the seed might fructify some day, but for the present " it sprung up quickly because it had no depth of earth." It is customary to think of the eighteenth century as somewhat limited in its scope ; but it is probable that no period ever offered so many counsels of perfection to men. In these days, when dietary questions have assumed a gravity which almost tempts us, against our better know-ledge, to transfer the mechanism of thought to the gastric regions, one laughs when one thinks of poets

mostly corpulent, and almost to a man self-indul-
gent, supplying texts to the vegetarians who now
preach with religious fervour the new *cultus* of St.
Cabbage.   Thackeray complains that his " Mrs. Spec "
considers cold mutton the natural food of man.   But
nothing seems to excite the disgust of the austere
epicures who loved turtle soup and *pâté-de-foie-gras*
whenever they could get it, so much as the fact that
man eats mutton.   It was all part of a general hypo-
crisy, innocent because too simple to deceive a baby.
The good lady who professed to discover from the
writings of Thomson, who was lazy, dirty, and luxurious, that he was an early riser, a " great swimmer and
rigorously abstinent," was clearly a soul sent pre-
maturely to earth ; she was meant to have been born
in the nineteenth century, somewhere near Rydal
Mount.   It was a widespread epidemic which we are
here noting.   There was so much make-believe in the
talk of all classes and callings that a man of downright
character like Johnson was apt to laugh at professions
of public sentiment of any kind.   Johnson said—
" When a butcher tells you that his heart bleeds for
his country, he has, in fact, no uneasy feeling."   These
were, according to him, notions that helped to amuse
the people, and keep off the *taedium vitae*.   Perhaps
a man who had seen the pressing dangers of '45 regarded by a menaced public with a mixture of supineness and curiosity, might be excused for holding firmly
to the opinion which he gave to Goldsmith for his
" Traveller " :

> " How small, of all that human hearts endure
> The part that laws or kings can cause or cure ! "

The American colonies, which he prophesied would never revolt, must have supplied him with uncomfortable evidence that in politics the gaseous may become solid ; the French Revolution, which taught the same lesson, he did not live to see. But his memory might furnish him with many facts to strengthen his views or prejudices as to the insignificance of sentimental discontents. In particular he knew exactly the practical value of declamations (including his own) against courtiers and pensioners ; he showed it by accepting a pension. Such generalities courtly circles could appraise like the rest of the world ; they could easily smile at a language which each man there might be employing in his turn. Thus Gay wrote his fables for the young Duke of Cumberland, the future "hero" of Culloden, whom, according to him, the nation saw—

> . . . "Grieve to hear distress
> And pant already to redress,"

and whom he reminds that—

> " Cowards are cruel ; but the brave
> Love mercy and delight to save ; "

and the freedom with which he talked about Court servilities and intrigues excited, Swift tells us, some comment ; but the Court itself, we are inclined to think, regarded all such *impersonal* satire as the merest effervescence ; no more likely to bias the mind of the young Prince than that early admonition to clemency was likely to touch his heart in after days. We quite believe that the post of Gentleman Usher to the little Princess Louisa, which Gay rejected with so much scorn, was by no means offered him as a slight, but rather as a recompense, which was considered to be nicely proportioned to the value of his counsels.

This plump Antaeus had no strength but when he touched earth ; no feebler verses were ever scribbled by any poet of name than his " Contemplation on Night," or " Thought on Eternity." But his character, if quite unsuited to these high themes, was amiable and affectionate, and the nearest approach to a work of genius which he left behind him is the description of the men he knew, as given in " Mr. Pope's Welcome from Greece." If Goldsmith's " Retaliation " did not come between us and this earlier poem, we should be more alive to the merits of Gay's genial and lively sketch. What obese and hearty people he makes strutting before us, with just a distinguishing touch here and there that we may know them apart ! Disney, with his queer exclamation, " Duke ! " invented, we suppose, to avoid profane swearing ; Jervas, the robust and debonair ; Dartneuf, gay joker :

> " And wondering Maine so fat, with laughing eyes
> (Gay, Maine, and Cheney, boon companions dear,
> Gay fat, Maine fatter, Cheney huge of size)."

Above all, visible as in a votive picture :

> " Honest, hatless Cromwell, with red breeches."

But it is time to take leave of Gay. We have said,

perhaps, more than enough to show that he was fortunate in his epoch, and that gifts such as his in our
day, when there is so much competition for the honour
of amusing us, would have given him a place much
lower than that which fortune has assigned him.   But,
if we cannot " beat our pensive bosoms " over him, as
Pope bids us on pain of being excluded from the
number of " the worthy and the good," we may, at
least, admit him to be worth a little more than the
flippant epitaph he composed for himself, and treat
his memory with the good-humoured indulgence
which his friends extended to his life.

OSSIAN AND HIS MAKER[1]

W E are convinced that the " Poems of Ossian " are a gigantic fraud. It is not necessary to know Gaelic, or to have studied even in translation the genuine relics of Gaelic poetry, to make this assertion. We will admit that there are real fragments of this poetry embedded here and there in the huge mass of Macpherson's publications. But we do not acquit a man of dishonesty because he passes a few good half-crowns amid hundreds of his own coinage. We know that this is a necessary trick of the game, and part of the prudential wisdom of knavery.

We do not say that Macpherson began with imposture. His reluctance (at Moffat in 1759) to translate, at the request of Home, the author of " Douglas," the few fragments of Erse song which he then professed to know, was probably quite genuine. It was innocent, as far as it arose from his own imperfect knowledge of Gaelic ; it was as objectionable as several other parts of his character, as far as it was due to his egregious vanity, and what he chose to call his " Highland pride, alarmed at appearing to the world only as a translator." We readily admit that the conceited lad thought that

[1] "Life and Letters of James Macpherson." Bailey Saunders. 1894.

the wretched rhymes he had already published, still-
born though they fell from the press, were a better
title to fame than honest pains bestowed upon the old
poetry of his native hills. The meagre results of
strictly *honest* work in this direction would never have
satisfied his soaring genius, and even when he' had
" translated " two epics he spoke of his achievement
with all the vainglory of original authorship.

We have Macpherson's own statements that of
old documents he had the smallest possible supply :
" Scarce any manuscript to be followed, except, indeed,
a very few mutilated ones in a kind of Saxon characters,
which was [as] utterly unknown to the Highlanders as
either the Greek or Hebrew letters." This is what he
says when, towards the end of his life, he is defending
his design of publishing his Gaelic "originals " in Greek
(!) characters. But we need scarcely quote his evidence
for a fact admitted by his apologists. It is, however,
of importance that what he himself meant by the
"originals " should be clearly ascertained. By his own
showing the great bulk of what he published as the
poems of Ossian was taken down from oral recitation.
By his own showing, therefore, when he talked of the
originals of " Fingal " and " Temora," he could not, in
honesty, have meant much more than manuscripts in
Gaelic, quite recently written, corresponding with the
English which he printed. Such manuscripts, even if
they were complete, and even if they corresponded
word for word with "Fingal," "Temora," "Berrathon,"
and all the rest, were absolutely worthless, as Johnson

declared, as evidence for the antiquity of these poems. We are giving nothing away if we admit that all the Gaelic of " Fingal " was on show in Becket's shop in this form "in the year 1762 for the inspection of the curious." The fact by itself does not even suffice to prove that Macpherson, or any of his correspondents, had heard any part of "Fingal" said or sung in the Highlands or the Hebrides.

It is not surprising that the public, however curious, made no response to the invitation to inspect in a bookseller's shop documents not three years old, utterly meaningless to the many who could not read them, and quite unconvincing to the few who could. That no one took the pains to visit the shop and discover, by ocular demonstration, that the evidence offered for "Fingal" there was nothing more than this, is a sign of an age not very searching in criticism of this kind. But that through this neglect judgment went by default we utterly deny. Judgment so far must be pronounced upon the *evidence ;* and it is the witness himself who, in effect, tells us that his evidence from written documents was worthless.

But even this worthless evidence was withheld for "Temora." The indifference of the public to the " originals " of " Fingal " made, according to Macpherson, any such pains to secure credit for his new venture superfluous. He therefore contented himself with publishing, with " Temora," a specimen of the Gaelic ; and for that purpose fixed upon the seventh book. We have a significant hint of the manner in which this specimen was produced. One of Macpherson's helpers was the Laird of Strathmashie, and of him Mr. Bailey Saunders tells us that—

"On his death in 1767 a manuscript is said to have been found amongst his papers, containing the Gaelic of the seventh book of 'Temora' in his handwriting, with numerous alterations and corrections, and headed 'First rude draft of the seventh book of "Temora."'"

Let us keep clearly in mind what we learn or infer from Macpherson himself as to the composition of this poem. It is made up almost entirely of fragments, taken down from recitation. These are placed by him in their proper sequence, and so combined that they form one narrative poem.[1] The epic thus formed is then divided by him into eight books. The division into books is the last stage in the process.

It was therefore when the work was structurally quite complete that Strathmashie was thus engaged upon it. And what had he before him? A complete seventh book in Gaelic, or a complete seventh book in English? If the manuscript was Gaelic that, and not *his* manuscript, was the "first rude draught." Nor could it have been so very "rude" after all. It consisted *ex hypothesi* of what had been so put

---

[1] There are lyric passages in the text of "Temora" obvious to any reader, and commented on by Macpherson. These lyric portions cannot amount to anything like a tenth part of the whole poem. But he claims that he had originals for *all the narrative part* of the epic as well, and in fact points out the difference in style, in the original, between the narrative and the lyric portions!

together by Macpherson himself that it made, in Gaelic, an intelligible section of a complete and intelligible story. If it is urged that the Gaelic as offered to Strathmashie was difficult, how had Macpherson been able to understand each separate fragment, and to assign it to its place in the epic? Macpherson was admittedly no good Gaelic scholar.[1] If he could understand his "originals" it was because they were easy to understand, and the alterations which an expert would need to make in the manuscript which Macpherson submitted to him would involve no great thought or trouble. This "first rude draft of the seventh book of Temora, with numerous alterations and corrections," can be reconciled only with one supposition. Strathmashie was making a translation from Macpherson's English. He was not revising, he was composing, the Gaelic. He was translating into a language, which, however well he may have known it, he could seldom have had occasion to write, and its literature consisted in reality only of a few scattered lyrics, with the phraseology of which he had to bring his version into some sort of harmony. His task was not unlike that of the good Greek scholars who year after year at Cambridge write a Greek ode after the

---

[1] He once, Mr. Saunders says, wanted to ask a bard whether he knew any poems about the Fingalians, but the words he used really meant, "Do the Fingalians owe you anything?" The man replied that if they did the bonds were lost, and he believed that any attempt to recover them at that time of day would be unavailing. Macpherson was foolish enough to be offended.

manner of Sappho, or the achievement of Professor
Jebb in rendering a poem of Browning's into the Greek
of Pindar.   Under such conditions, "numerous alterations and corrections" are inevitable even to the most
practised hands, before the composition is ready. We are
not surprised, therefore, that the Laird of Strathmashie's
manuscript bore evidences of great searchings of heart.
Nor is it wonderful that the published specimen contained, according to the Committee of the Highland
Society, some imperfections and modernisms.   If these
"modernisms" were in manuscripts made from recitation, which Macpherson handed to Strathmashie, what
becomes of the argument for the antiquity of Macpherson's Ossian, based upon the conservative vigour of
oral tradition in the Highlands?   And above all, the
bona fides of the translator being the question at stake,
what had he to do but to produce the Gaelic materials,
just as he received them or took them down, out of
which he constructed this seventh book?   He did
not, because he could not, do this.   If there were such
materials their very paucity would have convicted him
of fraud.

Mr. Bailey Saunders considers it very unlikely that
Macpherson could have written the twenty thousand
lines of Ossianic poems in the brief period of three and
a half years.   To us it is far more difficult to believe
that, however numerous his correspondents may have
been (and their number does not, perhaps, diminish
the difficulty), he collected in that brief period, mainly
from recitations heard in various parts of the High-

lands, the same great mass of *Gaelic*, translated all
that mass, after avowed disputes as to the meaning of
many passages, and found for each contribution its
exact place in a series of twenty-one poems, two of
which are epics, and almost all of which are tales, and
very coherent tales too, corresponding in structure,
with marvellous fidelity, to the arguments which Macpherson has prefixed to them.   Such a feat of con-
structive criticism has no parallel in literary history ;
it is the work of more than one lifetime ; that it should
have been so rapidly, yet so completely, performed,
transcends all belief.   In the alternative, that the great
bulk of these poems was of Macpherson's own composition, we see no difficulty whatever, after the publication of the "Fragments."   The real business was
to find or make legends, plots, episodes.   The great
Ossianic manner once formed could be reproduced *ad
infinitum*.   It was, in Hamlet's phrase, as easy as
lying ; to which, indeed, it bore no small resemblance.
We do not quite agree with Johnson that " many men,
many women, and many children could have written
Ossian."   But we certainly believe that many men,
and many women, given a few Gaelic names and a tale
to tell about them, could, after one perusal of " Fingal "
or " Temora," turn out a poem which, bating perhaps
the felicities which appear at very rare intervals in Macpherson's compilation, and prove that he had some
poetic gift, would pass for Macpherson-Ossianic.   Indeed, that excellent lady, Mrs. Ann Grant, of Laggan,
when, in 1788, she described with mingled delight and

horror Macpherson's return to his own country, had caught the style to perfection :

" The bard of bards," she writes, " who reached the mouldy harp of Ossian from the withered oak of Selma, and awakened the song of other times, is now moving, like a bright meteor, over his native hills ; and while the music of departed bards awakens the joy of grief, the spirits of departed warriors lean from their bright clouds to hear."

She could have gone on like that for ever, without being much more tedious than her original. In fact, nothing that we have ever come across rivals these poems for monotony ; in this we shall be contradicted by no one who has made, as we have made, the dreadful experiment of reading them from the first page to the last. The monotony is exactly what we should expect from a youth of excellent abilities, some poetic gift, and some reading, shrewd enough to know that to be safe he must not be venturesome, must avoid that sort of particularity which gives character and interest to old epic poetry, and which either proves the date of a poem or betrays the forger. Very seldom does Macpherson depart from the convenient vagueness in which he was secure. It was indeed somewhat venturesome to make his Ossian talk of Caracul (for Caracalla) four years before that nickname was given, and though it was urged by Dr. Whittaker, in general no partisan of Macpherson, that the poet would naturally speak of a man by the name by which he came to be generally known, this apology is scarcely satisfactory. The defeat of Caracul is in part the theme of Comala, one of the most extravagant and impossible of the shorter poems; a piece dramatic in structure, including five "persons" and a chorus of bards; and we remark, in passing, that it seems highly improbable that it should have been obtained, in its present form, from recitation. "This poem," Macpherson tells us, "is valuable on account of the light it throws on the antiquity of Ossian's compositions. The Caracul mentioned here is the same with Caracalla, the son of Severus, who in the year 211 commanded an expedition against the Caledonians." Now, early in this very year (February 4) Severus *died* at York; and from the poem it appears that he was still alive at the date of the battle; we infer, therefore, that "the son of the king of the world" made this invasion beyond the northernmost limits of the empire, and sustained a crushing defeat, *in the depth of winter*, and this, too, at the very crisis of his fortunes, his father dying, and his brother and rival Geta, the favourite of the soldiers whose lives were thus rashly thrown away. That Roman history should know nothing of such an event at such a time, nay, that the succession to the empire should not have been affected by it, is a very remarkable circumstance. That Severus was preparing for a summer campaign against the Caledonians when his career was cut short by death is another fact which renders this premature expedition altogether incredible. We may, therefore, safely infer that at any rate Macpherson's A.D. 211 must be wrong. It may be urged that though Macpherson was so far in error, the

poem may refer to a previous campaign.   To this the
best answer is the poem itself, of which Macpherson
has perfectly interpreted the drift.   It speaks of the
defeat of the Romans as a final deliverance, which
caused "the wings of their pride" to "spread in other
lands." We may dismiss with contempt, or something
worse, Macpherson's impudent pretence that this name
"Caracul" establishes the antiquity of his Ossian. Yet
no other pretence is tenable.   Ossian is describing a
victory won by his own father.   The name of the
defeated prince could not be for him derived from
historic literature.   And even if we attribute the poem
to some later bard,—if among barbarous tribes *penitus
toto divisos orbe*, the name of a hostile leader survives,
it is because it has been caught from contact with the
invaders and retained in a form more or less corrupt.
That the name "Caracalla" could never have been
heard, or thus transmitted, by the victorious barbarians,
has been shown.   If, therefore, Caracul is Caracalla, it
would be hard to fix for "Comala" a date at all compatible with the remote antiquity claimed for that poem ;
we must trace it to the dawn of historic study in the
North.   But be it remembered that, as Blair says, these
poems must be anterior to the establishment of the clan
system (itself very ancient), for they contain no mention of it.   This is a perfectly true inference from their
contents ; and therefore Macpherson was more saga-
cious than some of his defenders in claiming for them
a very early date, and attributing them to Ossian himself.   He committed himself, however, in this instance

by being too *particular*. He justifies exactly the suspicion Gray derived from his letters, which were, he
says, "calculated (one would imagine) to deceive, and
yet not cunning enough to do it cleverly." [1]

It would be interesting could we know more of the
way in which Macpherson dealt with the few old
documents that came into his hands. We can quite
believe that "he parted very reluctantly with whatever he had succeeded in obtaining." One or two
ancient manuscripts were a very necessary addition to
the display of evidence in Becket's shop. But beyond
the statement of Mr. Macneill, Minister of Hovemore,
in South Uist, that "the original of 'Berrathon' was
contained in an important manuscript which, with
three or four more, Macmhuirid in his presence gave
to Macpherson, who bound himself in writing to return
them," we have found nothing in Mr. Bailey Saunders's
book to connect old MSS. with Macpherson's Ossian.
Of the value of this testimony our readers are as competent as ourselves to judge. What was the antiquity
of the "important" manuscript, and how far it cor-

---

[1] It was urged that "caracul" really means in Gaelic "fierce-
eyed," and that Macpherson was only mistaken in identifying
the name with Caracalla. If there was a "son of the king of
the world" known to his contemporary Ossian as "Caracul,"
and afterwards called in another part of the world, and with a
perfectly different signification, "Caracalla," the coincidence is
certainly startling. It is scarcely necessary to say that by
Ossian is meant Macpherson's Ossian, the Ossian in whom
Macpherson believed, the Ossian whose date he approximately
assigned, the contents of all the Ossianic poems published by
him squaring far better with that "floruit" than with any other.

responded with " Berrathon," are, we suppose, questions now beyond solution. But an extract supplied by Mr. Saunders, from the journal of John Mackenzie, on July 22, in the year (apparently) 1789, may assist our judgment a little :

" Went at one o'clock to Putney-common, to Mr. Macpherson. He said he had been searching in an old trunk upstairs, which he had with him in East Florida, for the original of ' Berrathon.' That he feared it was in an imperfect condition, and that part of it was wanting, as of ' Carthon ' ; that he had only put together a few lines of it, and those not to his own liking ; that he had tired of it after a short sitting."

We suppose that this was not the "important manuscript " itself which Macpherson had bound himself in writing to "return." On any hypothesis, however, we find by " combining," as the editor of the " Eatanswill Gazette" would say, " our information," that the English of "Berrathon" lacks any sort of warrant. Another fact of very distinct significance Mr. Saunders relegates to a footnote. He tells us in the text that the Macdonalds had great difficulty in getting back from Macpherson the "Red Book" upon which the family set great store. But we learn also from the note on p. 131 that Campbell, of Islay, who examined this book in 1873, "found no poem in it which could be the original of any part of Macpherson's Ossian."

It would be tedious, even if we had space, to produce all the indications which these pages afford, pointing to one and the same conclusion. We are

simply amazed at the facility with which, up to the
first years of the present century, every one at all
deeply interested in the subject, except, perhaps, David
Hume and Gray, assisted, unwittingly, at a great
process of concoction. Even John Mackenzie, who,
as secretary of the Highland Society, might have
known his real duty better, seems to have virtually
helped (by way of furnishing "originals") to turn
Macpherson's English into Gaelic ; and Blair, who
was Macpherson's great voucher with the British
public, and professed to have seen him at work,
laboured, according to his *protégé*, under "much want
of information on the subject" when he opposed the
project of printing the Gaelic in Greek characters, and
by his own acknowledgment knew nothing of that
language. To make the good or ill fortune of Macpherson's evidences complete, we are told that his
MS., at one time in the Advocates' library, unaccount-
ably disappeared, and that his diary, "which is said to
have contained some information as to the collection
of the poems, was stolen, probably by a servant, shortly
after Sir David Brewster's death in 1868."

Strangely as John Mackenzie himself went to work,
it is perfectly clear that the Highland Society, though
their conclusions were timidly and feebly expressed,
could, only forty years after Macpherson's labours,
find no such connected tales as he published, nothing
in fact but fragmentary lyrics—of which no one
questions that he made some use. That they found
" no one poem the same in title and tenour with his

publications" is unaccountable if we are to believe
that *he* found, even for his many shorter poems, the
raw material of coherent fables; for even when the
body of a song is lost, the last thing to perish is some
indication of its general drift. Moreover, Macpherson's defenders are inconsistent with themselves in
attributing such great effects to the official discourage-
ment of Gaelic. The tenacious patriotism which
could retain through many centuries the substance
(bating the necessary links) of twenty thousand lines,
could scarcely, in forty years, have so far yielded to
foreign pressure as to retain no vestige of those
memories except in a few fragments.

Again, we differ from Mr. Saunders, inasmuch as
we believe that Macpherson, with his "Highland
pride," reveals clearly enough his ambition, even in
connection with Ossian, to figure as an original genius.
What else is to be made of such expressions as
these?—

"Without vanity I say it, I think I could write tolerable
poetry; and I assure my antagonists that I should not translate what I could not imitate." "A translator who cannot
equal his original is incapable of expressing its beauties."

What is the "profound truth" which Mr. Saunders
supposes this second sentence to contain? Taken by
itself it is either false or a mere truism. If it means
that none should translate a poet but those who can
rival him in creative power, it means that Homer and
Dante should have remained untranslated. Interpreted
by the *first* sentence, *and* by the high place on Par-

nassus which Macpherson gives to his Ossian, its significance becomes quite plain. It is Macpherson's way of telling the world, " These are works of unrivalled genius, but I could rival them if I pleased." Conscious that he was the real author of efforts which passed for sublime, he was specially galled by a defence of their genuineness, based on his supposed incompetence to produce them ; and he coveted the honour and glory of a poet of the first rank, without the odium which attached to those literary rascals, his countrymen Bower and Lauder.

We cannot agree with Mr. Saunders that there is "as good a case for the authenticity of the Ossianic poems as for that of the Edda or the Nibelungenlied," but if we could believe that " the old writers who gave those works to the world " had only the same *quantum* of material as came into the hands of Macpherson we should still question, from a moral point of view, his title to rank with them. Every writer has a duty to his age, and to the standard of candour and fidelity which his own generation prescribes ; and Macpherson's was an age critical in everything except—and it was a lucky exception for him—the skill of the expert in detecting imposture.[1] Though he never could have become so

---

[1] This is advisedly written. Psalmanazar, Bower, Lauder, were *clumsy* impostors, and it required no great *skill* to detect them. That part of the confutation of Chatterton which is based upon a knowledge of the earlier stages of our language belongs in the main to the present century. That there should have been so much of this sort of brigandage in the eighteenth century indicates an inefficient police.

important a figure as he thought himself, we are convinced that he would have achieved a fame in literature quite as great and much less sinister if he had
been more honest.   His promise must not be esti-
mated by his early rhymes ; for these are Aberdonian.
Yet they are not a whit worse than Thomson's, at the
same period of life.   Of his blank verse, Mr. Saunders
tells us that " it betrays the study of classical models
rather than any capacity for direct observation," but
this is precisely what we have noted in several de-
scriptive passages in Ossian, otherwise sufficiently
striking, which seem to betray themselves by a certain
incongruity.   Be that as it may, when in "The Hunter"
Macpherson writes:

> ". . . Now and then the breathing breezes sigh
> Through the half-quivering leaves, and, far removed,
> The sea rolls feeble murmurs to the shore "—

we have just the sort of scenic effect in which his
Ossian abounds.   And let any one read that fragment
of a Norse tale which in his Preface (1773) Macpherson first gives in his Ossianic prose, and then in
the conventional rhymed heroics of his day and it will
be seen with what facility he could pass from the one
manner to the other.   He is probably at his best in
some dramatic touches, such as he perhaps really
found in the fragment that fascinated Gray—

> "Are these his groans in the gale?
> Is this his broken boat on the shore?"

or such as he more probably invented in "Croma":

"I gave my arm to the (blind) king; he felt it with his aged hands. The sigh rose in his breast, and his tears came down. 'Thou art strong, my son,' he said, 'but not like the King of Morven.'"

We are not inclined to depreciate the abilities of any man who could so notably influence the literature of Europe, and captivate for a while the greatest European minds. Whatever was the source of Macpherson's imagery, he gave it for a time the charm of novelty, and, floated on the stream of romance, his large but unsubstantial craft carried a little valuable freight. We do indeed suspect that the "*sounding* shells," of which he had so plentiful a stock, are nothing but the classic *testudo* adopted by him for a drinking-vessel; but now and then he has fared better with his merchandise; his heroes for example who "hum surly songs" may be the musical ancestors of the Roundhead in Tennyson's "Talking Oak." Though it was not, *pace* Mrs. Barrett Browning, "mountain winds that swelled out" Ossian's vest, but in the main the breath of James Macpherson, that breath had some little power. Some permanent results of the Ossianic movement may be traced even in the later literature which boasted a complete emancipation from its influence. His besetting sin is, as we have said, monotony; there is a terrible facility for the young poet in dealing with the elementary forces of nature, and, if he is encouraged, he is certain to abuse it; even the sun in such hands palls upon us, and before we close "Ossian," we have a perfectly Satanic hatred of his beams. Yet the fault itself, under all the circumstances, was necessary to an ephemeral success, for that which is fragmentary has but little vogue; and one of the lessons of this strange episode in the history of literature is that the world, even the discerning world, is influenced by mere volume, and receives impressions not only of the reason but of the imagination, by dint of much repetition.

COVENTRY PATMORE [1]

I N these volumes we may study one of the most striking apparent contrasts which English literature has ever exhibited. Whether the contrast will please or not will depend, in a measure at any rate, upon the bias and temperament of the reader; but the critic will find his first and perhaps his principal pleasure in noting it, and drawing from it such instruction as he may.

It is possible that many of those who know Coventry Patmore mainly, if not only, as the author of the " Angel in the House," have inferred that the genius which lavished its wealth so profusely upon the felicities of domestic life was capable of a more ambitious theme.   Not of course that we are inclined to disparage a subject which, as long as it is the poet's function to discourse—

" Of man, of nature, and of human life,"

must be one of the very worthiest.   But in this instance we recognize a self-imposed limitation; a range of thought and feeling conditioned by the surroundings of a particular and highly cultivated class.   These re-

[1] Coventry Patmore. Poetical Works. 2 vols. 1886.

finements upon emotions themselves refined belong to
a society carefully guarded from the troubles and
dangers which are necessary to heroic action or passion.
Censorious criticism calls the " Idylls of the King " a
boudoir epic ; but the term belongs less unquestionably
to the " Angel in the House " and " The Victories of
Love." The *boudoir* epic of the last century was " The
Rape of the Lock," and we are conscious of a growth
in seriousness and a changed conception of the function
of poetry, when we reflect that we now demand some
moral purpose from our poets even when their material
is most artificial and luxurious.

It will seem to some readers a sort of sacrilege to
bring such poems as Coventry Patmore's into any
relation with the obsolete literature of satire and
badinage. Yet their epigrammatic character is certainly
a heritage from a very different past. With a position
almost unique in literature, and with a strong character
of originality, Coventry Patmore nevertheless is what
he is partly by wide and careful study. Sometimes,
indeed, not only the art, but the thought itself, is
borrowed. The lines in "Tamerton Church Tower":

> "A Mary in the house of God,
> A Martha in her own,"

have long ago passed into a proverb. Few people, we
imagine, know that this beautiful epigram has been
passed on to our poet through the frivolous hands
of Horace Walpole, who found an epitaph ending
" Mundo Martha, Maria Deo." Yet the thought,

however he came by it, belongs to Coventry Patmore of right, so germane is it to that faculty of antithesis in which he is a consummate master, and which he exercises generally with great refinement and little exaggeration.

We have spoken of a self-imposed limitation in Coventry Patmore's work. The power of seizing and describing character which he exercises, within those limits, in his earlier poems gave promise of the sympathetic treatment of character in a wider choice from all sorts and conditions of men. At least the faculty was *there ;* the bar to its use would be, if anything, the lack of the same interest in men in the mass. Now, the lower classes of society, as far as they appear at all in the "Angel in the House," bask in the rays reflected upon them by their social superiors. As long as they remain in this *quasi*-feudal relation they are respectable, though ungrammatical, objects of interest. The prattle of the housekeeper faithfully represents this character :

> "Well, Mr. Felix, Sir, I'm sure
>   The morning's gone off excellent !
> I never saw the show to pass
>   The ladies, in their fine fresh gowns
> So sweetly dancing on the grass
>   To music with its ups and downs.
> We'd such work, Sir, to clean the plate," etc.

Here a certain graphic power is observable—the same power which we notice in "The Girl of All Periods" and "Olympus"—but conditioned here by

the form and subject of the poem. The question
which Coventry Patmore's subsequent writings suggest
is whether his sympathies are not permanently hampered by the prejudice of class. With refined thought,
and *wide* sympathies, and the poet's eye for the world
of nature, we should have the elements of great poetry
ready to hand. What is it then that makes us feel
that "The Unknown Eros," etc., so great a contrast,
as we said at the outset, to Coventry Patmore's earlier
poems, as belonging more distinctly to the literature
of power, falls short of the same measure of success in
its own province? His theme, in both of its main
aspects, is a noble one; comparable, indeed, to Dante's.
He has his Florence and his Beatrice; his degenerate
countrymen; his earthly love foreshadowing a love
celestial and ideal. Dante is an evidence that it is
possible for genius to make political and even personal
antipathies immortal. But Dante has done this by a
faculty quite independent of the passion which sets it
to work; the man "who had seen hell," and Purgatory
to boot, had a tremendous machinery at his command.
He does not succeed by making us share his animosi-
ties; rather the terror and pity which he excites are
all in the interest of his victims. We care nothing for
the merits of Guelph or Ghibelline, or the sins of Pope
Nicolas III. or Boniface VIII.; the excessive partiality
of Simon of Tours for the eels of Bolsena has but a
curious interest for us. There is, besides, in Dante,
always something of the judicial tone; and he con-
demns his dearest friends to the severest penal fires.

But a modern poet, with a kindred intensity of conviction, has an uphill task if his readers are not at the
outset in sympathy with him.   The commencement
of the poem " 1867 "—

> " In the year of the great crime
> When the false English Nobles and their Jew,
> By God demented, slew
> The Trust they stood twice pledged to keep from wrong "—

which has appended to it the note :

> " In this year the middle and upper classes were disfran-
> chised by Mr. Disraeli's Government, and the final destruc-
> tion of the liberties of England by the Act of 1884 rendered
> inevitable "—

is the statement of a particular view of very modern
politics, a statement crude in itself, and needing an
explanation, which, however, is cruder still ; a direct
slap in the face to perhaps two-thirds of Coventry
Patmore's readers, by way of encouraging them to do
justice to what follows.   This is a drawback to which
the poet himself is something less than indifferent ;
we, who are but looking on, and trying to estimate his
work on purely critical grounds, cannot but see that it
is a drawback of a very serious kind.   For the indignation that finds its vent in poetry must interest us
either because we share it, or because it makes appeal
to a moral truth deeper than the occasion which
excites it, or because it is manifested in the plastic
power of a great imagination, presenting scenes which
fascinate us when judgment and sympathy are inert

or even adverse. Thus the Hebrew Prophet lives still, as the witness to a righteousness independent of time and place, for those who have a very imperfect acquaintance, or no acquaintance at all, with the circumstances of his mission ; Dante lives because his Heaven and Hell and Purgatory have been made almost visible to our eyes, and he has made us believe for a while that what we have seen there are the judgments of God, little as we care now for Dante's opinions, his loves or hates ; even Juvenal, though we are quite indifferent to the character of Domitian, will live as long as men continue to read with pleasure the proceedings of the council gathered round the gigantic turbot, and can admire the fierce burst of scorn with which that scene is closed. What conditions of success analogous to these does Coventry Patmore start with ? When the decadence of England is a fact manifest to all men, how many will attribute it precisely to "the disfranchisement of the upper and middle classes by Mr. Disraeli's Government in 1867, and the final destruction of the liberties of England by the Act of 1884"? And yet that this, and nothing but this, is the explanation of our downfall, Coventry Patmore assures us, in a passage which we will quote at length, because it seems to us to summarize his political creed :

"Ah, Land once mine
That seem'd to me too sweetly wise,
Too sternly fair for aught that dies,
Past is thy proud and pleasant state,
That recent date

M

When, strong and single, in thy sovereign heart,
The thrones of thinking, hearing, sight,
The cunning hand, the knotted thew
Of lesser powers that heave and hew,
And each the smallest beneficial part,
And merest pore of breathing, beat
Full and complete,
The great pulse of thy generous might,
Equal in inequality,
That soul of joy in low and high ;
When not a churl but felt the Giant's heat,
Albeit he simply call'd it his,
Flush in his common labour with delight,
And not a village-maiden's kiss
But was for this
More sweet,
And not a sorrow but did lightlier sigh
And for its private self less greet,
The whilst that other so majestic self stood by!
Integrity so vast could well afford
To wear in working many a stain
To pillory the cobbler vain
And license madness in a lord.
On that were all men well agreed;
And, if they did a thing,
Their strength was with them in their deed,
And from amongst them came the shout of a king."

The corruptions by which a nation is ruined are of long standing, and particular enactments are their consequences and not their causes. If we understand this passage aright, up to a recent date all Englishmen were agreed that the integrity secured by the governing classes could safely tolerate the excesses of the aristocracy, whilst it punished the free expression of opinion on the part of the artisan. It would be easy to dis-

prove the fact of this *consensus* of opinion ; still easier
to expose a theory so crude as this, or to denounce a
moral standard so ignoble and invertebrate. But it is
sufficient to say that no *great* poetry can be built upon
such a foundation ; that the theme being what it is, all
the art, were it ten times as great as it is, employed in
embellishing it would be worse than thrown away.
The topic is worthy of the political and literary capacity
of Theodore Hook ; the morality would have been
warmly applauded by the followers of the Prince
Regent. When greater gifts are enlisted in such a
service we can only exclaim with Jaques, " O knowledge ill-inhabited, worse than Jove in a thatched
house ! " Let the poet regret, if he pleases, the trans-
ference of power ; let him anticipate, by representing
as already full-grown, the evils which every change
accomplished without social convulsion, only gradually
develops ; let him idealize the past, and put a *nimbus*
round the heads of the privileged few, and he may
compel our admiration, if not our assent ; but it is an
artistic blunder of the worst kind to foist the mad but
licensed lord and the conceited and pilloried cobbler
into this goodly company ; to mingle harsh realities
with pleasant fictions, to tempt us to dream and
suddenly shake us up to think. It is as if some
unkind hand were to introduce into Mr. Dicksee's
" Passing of Arthur " the sketch of a Mohawk fighting
a watchman. And who can help reflecting, at our
poet's instigation, that the stains here noted as accidental and negligable were radical defects in our

"vast integrity"; that he who tells the now "out-
lawed Best":

> "Know 'twas the force of function high
> In corporate exercise, and public awe
> Of Nature's, Heaven's, and England's law
> That Best, though mixed with Bad, should reign
> Which kept you in your sky!"

should be the last to suggest that a system based upon
this principle could afford to license a contempt of that
virtue which is its very essence?   The naïve revelation
of a class-feeling at the very point where a lofty
morality should supersede it deprives these poetical
jeremiads of any weight or impressiveness ; they are
Latter-day Pamphlets in which spleen and bitter contempt, and a prejudice essentially vulgar, have usurped
the place of moral earnestness. Rhadamanthus, though
his methods are not ours, though, as Virgil tells us, he
first punishes and then hears, may be an august and
venerable figure ; but a Rhadamanthus in plush in-
spires no reverence or respect.

Compare for a moment Coventry Patmore with a
poet whom we should credit with less imaginative
power.   Cowper's theme is also often the decadence
of England ; and, whilst we do not call " Expostula-
tion," or " Truth," or the " Progress of Error " great
poems, we maintain that they possess the essential
character of prophecy, in attacking corruption at its
root and source ; and that the cardinal error of de-
ploring change whilst palliating the servile toleration
of vice in high places, which must always make change

at last inevitable, was an error from which taste and good sense and deep conviction kept Cowper wholly free.

We could easily show by quotations that the feeling which we here note is predominant in these poems ; but that it is really characteristic will be manifest from this, that it makes its appearance in a region of thought where we should least of all expect it, and where it is even shockingly incongruous. The worship of the Virgin Mother will have, let us admit it freely, a fascination for the human spirit as long as gentleness, compassion, purity, and all the other graces that contribute to form the ideal of perfect womanhood can thus be enshrined and hallowed. The range of poetry is not circumscribed by doctrine, and it is not always the poetry of Roman Catholicism—often in this direction rhapsodical and sensuous—that has presented this worship in its most attractive light for thoughtful and cultivated minds. And certainly we know no parallel to the strange mixture of celestial ecstasy and very mundane scorn which Coventry Patmore offers us in such poems as " The Child's Purchase." He seems to have taken as his model the tone and sentiment of " Sir Lob " in " Tamerton Church Tower " :

> " I hate the herd that vulgar be
> And, O, the stars are fair ! "

Surely, no loose, unlettered hind of Paganism ever praised the gods more amiss than this Christian and cultivated poet, for whom the parable of the Pharisee

and the Publican would seem to be a dead letter.   Let
us hear him :

> " Chief stone of stumbling ; sign built in the way
> To set the foolish everywhere a-bray ;
> Hem of God's robe, which all who touch are heal'd ;
> To which the outside Many honour yield
> With a reward and grace
> Unguess'd by the unwash'd boor that hails Him to His face,
> Spurning the safe, ingratiant courtesy
> Of suing Him by thee ;
> *Ora pro me !* "

We despair of representing in words the impression
which this sad medley of blessing and cursing has
made upon us.   We have said that we know no parallel
to it.   We beg pardon ; the parallel is to be found in
the last lines of Browning's " Soliloquy of the Spanish
Cloister,"

> " 'St, there's vespers ! *Plena gratia*
> *Ave, Virgo !* Gr—r—r, you swine ! "

There are other poems in the same series—" Eros
and Psyche," " De Natura Deorum," and " Psyche's
Discontent "—the ethical scope and poetic value of
which we feel quite unable to discern, and of which
therefore the less said by us the better.   There are
again poems more within our compass, the pessimistic
tone of which we find it hard to reconcile with any
Christian creed.   Such is the short poem, " Magna est
Veritas " :

> " Here in this little bay,
> Full of tumultuous life and great repose,
> Where, twice a day,
> The purposeless, glad ocean comes and goes,

Under high cliffs, and far from the huge town,
I sit me down.
For want of me the world's course will not fail :
When all its work is done, the lie shall rot ;
The truth is great, and shall prevail,
When none cares whether it prevail or not."

It is pleasant to turn from these to those poems in which, in spite of a certain fierce exaggeration, we discover a true corrective and guiding principle. As in this from " The Two Deserts," which quaintly enforces a favourite theme of our poet's, the happiness of limitation :

" Put by the Telescope !
Better without it man may see,
Stretch'd awful in the hush'd midnight,
The ghost of his eternity.
Give me the nobler glass that swells to the eye
The things which near us be,
Till science rapturously hails,
In the minutest water-drop,
A torment of innumerable tails.
These at the least do live.
But rather give
A mind not much to pry
Beyond our royal-fair estate
Betwixt these deserts blank of small and great.
Wonder and beauty our own courtiers are,
Pressing to catch our gaze,
And out of obvious ways
Ne'er wandering far."

And certainly we have never met with anything in literature more full of a pathetic *desiderium* than the poem called " Departure," more instinct with tenderness and compassion for the heart of childhood than the " Toys." These things will live, for it is the universally human which prevails in poetry, and through this alone can poetry give weight to prejudices in their own nature personal or ephemeral. In as far as the poet forgets this he succeeds in spite of himself, and only by virtue of that divine gift which no perverse use can make altogether fruitless.

ENGLAND'S HELICON
MORE LYRICS FROM ELIZABETHAN
SONG-BOOKS
SIDNEY'S ASTROPHEL AND STELLA

THE rich abundance of imagery, the copious vocabulary, the varied music of the Elizabethan time was a common possession. These gifts, all or some, belonged to men not remarkable for depth of thought—to writers who had "more copie than weight," but who were possessed of that quick eye for resemblances and analogies which the author of "Euphues" exhibits even more strikingly than the author of "Hamlet." What is still more noticeable, they belong to men who are in literature only the shadow of a shade—who, though they were themselves—

"Faithful prophets who spake as beseemed the god and his shrine,"

have hardly escaped that long night which buries those who have had no sacred bard to sing their praises. How many, beyond the privileged circle of professed students of literature, have heard, for instance, of

Edmund Bolton? Yet Edmund Bolton could write
thus :

"As withereth the primrose by the river,
As fadeth summer's-sun from gliding fountains,
As vanisheth the light-blown bubble ever,
As melteth snow upon the mossy mountains ;
So melts, so vanisheth, so fades, so withers,
The rose, the shine, the bubble and the snow
Of praise, pomp, glory, joy (which short life gathers),
Fair praise, vain pomp, sweet glory, brittle joy.
The withered primrose by the mourning river,
The faded summer's-sun from weeping fountains,
The light-blown bubble vanished for ever,
The molten snow upon the naked mountains,
   Are emblems that the treasures we uplay
   Soon wither, vanish, fade, and melt away.

"For as the snow, whose lawn did over-spread
Th' ambitious hills, which giant-like did threat
To pierce the heavens with their aspiring head,
Naked and bare doth leave their craggy seat ;
When as the bubble, which did empty fly
The dalliance of the undiscernèd wind,
On whose calm rolling winds it did rely,
Hath shipwreck made, where it did dalliance find ;
And when the sunshine which dissolved the snow,
Coloured the bubble with a pleasant vary,
And made the rathe and timely primrose grow,
Swarth clouds withdrawn (which longer time do tarry)—
   Oh what is praise, pomp, glory, joy, but so
   As shine by fountains, bubbles, flowers, or snow ?"

Shakespeare himself, we are tempted to say, could
scarcely have written finer lines than—

"Th' ambitious hills, which giant-like did threat
To pierce the heavens with their aspiring head,"

or—

"The dalliance of the undiscernèd wind."

And that eclectic method, favoured by Matthew Arnold, which assumes that the great masters of song could put into a single phrase a note of distinction by which they may be recognized, is hopelessly ship-wrecked against such instances, which, coming in fact from those who are least in fame, might well have come from the very greatest. And who is "Ignoto" who subscribes that lovely invocation of the "Shepherd to his Flowers":

"Your honours of the flowery meads I pray
You pretty daughters of the earth and sun"?

Not Ralegh, as Mr. Bullen assures us, and, therefore, possibly one of those many other men of practical endeavour at this time, over whose life's course the spirit of poetry breathed not as a trade-wind, but as an occasional zephyr. One great fascination of col-lections such as "England's Helicon," or the "Lyrics from Elizabethan Song-books," of Mr. Bullen, is the suggestion of an undercurrent of genius, to which nothing now testifies but the bubbles on the surface; of a tribe of intellectual, but somewhat lazy giants, who bore about with them in court or camp great powers for the most part dormant or inert, but displayed upon occasion with as much vigour and facility as if they were in constant exercise. It is an age in which literature has not yet acquired the traditions of a craft, an age in which none are experts, but all are experi-mentalists, and the drama alone is moulded and con-ditioned by popular appeal. The scholar and courtier

has, at such a time, every advantage, except that signal
advantage which a solicitude for posthumous fame
can alone secure.   If Shakespeare himself had little or
nothing to do with gathering together "his sugred
sonnets among his private friends," how many men
even more careless and with less expectation than his
that—

> " Not marble nor the gilded monuments
> Of princes, shall outlive this powerful rime,"

may have sunk in those shipwrecks of time, after which,
in Landor's phrase, "hen-coops and empty barrels
bob upon the surface under a serene and smiling sky,
while the graven or depicted images of the gods are
scattered on invisible rocks "?

Our Edmund Bolton has hardly escaped "on broken
pieces" to land.   We confess to knowing nothing
more about him than Mr. Bullen tells us, or his own
unconscious revelation of himself in his verse suggests.
" One of the most learned men of his time," he wrote
"The Elements of Armories," and an interesting treatise
called "Hypercritica."   He accompanied Buckingham
on his journey to Spain in 1623.   He "laboured to
establish a Royal Academy or College of Honour 'for
the breeding and bringing-up of the nobility and gentry
of this kingdom.' "   We might conjecture that in social
status and intellectual mould he resembled Spenser—
more fortunate than Spenser in his life, but less secure
of immortality.   A certain sad dignity belongs to his
style even in his lighter hour of song.   He is religious
also, and we should like to believe that the author of

the beautiful Carol on the Nativity was a precursor of
Milton in the spirit as well as in the letter:

> "'For lo ! the world's great Shepherd now is born,
> A blessed babe, an infant full of power ;
> After long night uprisen is the morn,
> Renowning Bethlem in the Saviour.
> > Sprung is the perfect day
> > By prophets seen afar ;
> > Sprung is the mirthful May
> > Which winter cannot mar.'
> In David's city doth this sun appear,
> Clouded in flesh ; yet, shepherds, sit we here ?" [1].

We owe to Mr. Bullen the rescue from oblivion of a
remarkable poem by some unknown master-hand, the
reading of which has had much to do with our reflections upon the uncertainty of literary fame.   We
are not surprised that Mr. Bullen writes, "I doubt
whether it would be possible for me to have lost
memory of that poem if I had ever seen it in print.
Verse so stately, so simple, so flawless is not lightly
forgotten."   We suspect him of wonder that so noble a

---

[1] We have assumed with Mr. Bullen that "E. B." in "England's
Helicon" is always Edmund Bolton, although his name is only
once subscribed in full.   It would not be a less suggestive fact
if "E. B." were quite unknown to us.   There is a "W. S." in
"England's Helicon," who is not William Shakespeare but
William Smith, author of "Chloris ; or, the Complaint of the
Passionate Despised Shepherd," 1596.   The initials, W. S.,
have been a prolific source of error, not always, we may conjecture, undesigned.   Besides standing for William Shakespeare,
they have stood for William Smith and perhaps for Wentworth
Smith, and, according to Mr. Fleay, for Shakespeare's brother
actor, William Sly.

poem could have been so long unknown ; perhaps even of doubt whether the case is really so.   We, at any rate, shall have no right to censure him, if this treasure which he unearths from the Christ Church MSS. should prove to be of less obscure origin than he supposes.   It was set to music by John Ford ; the abruptness of the opening either indicates that it is a fragment, or belongs to the dramatic character which marks it throughout :

"Yet if his majesty, our sovereign lord,
Should of his own accord
Friendly himself invite,
And say, ' I'll be your guest to-morrow night,'
How should we stir ourselves, call and command
All hands to work !   ' Let no man idle stand.
Set me fine Spanish tables in the hall,
See they be fitted all ;
Let there be room to eat,
And order taken that there want no meat.
See every sconce and candlestick made bright,
That without tapers they may give a light.
Look to the presence : are the carpets spread,
The daïs o'er the head,
The cushions in the chairs,
And all the candles lighted on the stairs ?
Perfume the chambers, and in any case
Let each man give attendance in his place.'
Thus if the King were coming would we do,
And 'twere good reason too ;
For 'tis a duteous thing
To show all honour to an earthly King,
And after all our travail and our cost,
So he be pleased, to think no labour lost.
But at the coming of the King of Heaven

All's set at six and seven :
We wallow in our sin,
Christ cannot find a chamber in the inn.
We entertain Him always like a stranger,
And as at first still lodge Him in the manger."

The religious poet, we know, is at this time seldom so dignified when he moves with so much life as he does here—a quibble is the Cleopatra for which he must be content to lose the ear of a modern world less disposed to be " punned into salvation." Here, for instance, is a bard we doubt not as earnest as Herbert, but with more than Herbert's quaintness :

" My sins are like the hairs upon my head,
    And raise their audit to as high a score.
In this they differ : *they* do daily shed,
    But ah my sins grow daily more and more :
If by my hairs thou number out my sins,
Heaven make me bald before that day begins."

But sometimes the touch of quaintness is more gentle, and the thought developed is more than an idle play of fancy, as in this (from John Danyel's " Songs for the Lute, Viol, and Voice," 1606):

" If I could shut the gate against my thoughts
    And keep out sorrow from this room within,
Or memory could cancel all the notes
    Of my misdeeds, and I unthink my sin :
How free, how clear, how clean my soul should lie,
Discharged of such a loathesome company !

Or were there other rooms without my heart
    That did not to my conscience join so near,
Where I might lodge the thoughts of sin apart
    That I might not their clam'rous crying hear ;

What peace, what joy, what ease should I possess,
Freed from the horrors that my soul possess !

But O my Saviour, Who my refuge art,
    Let Thy dear mercies stand 'twixt them and me,
And be the wall to separate my heart
    So that I may at length repose me free ;
That peace, and joy, and rest may be within,
And I remain divided from my sin."

If we prefer the serious muse, it is because she tells or suggests more than her lighter-minded sisters. For instance, how well the following *memento mori*, with its

" *Vivat Eliza* for an *Ave Mary* "

discloses the story of one who has lived on through shifting and hazardous times into a changed world :

" Time's eldest son, Old Age (the heir of ease,
    Strength's foe, Love's woe, and foster to devotion)
Bids gallant Youth in martial prowess please ;
    As for himself, he has no earthly motion,
But thinks sighs, tears, vows, prayers, and sacrifices
As good as shows, masques, jousts, or tilt-devices.
Then sit thee down and say thy *Nunc Dimittis*
    With *De Profundis, Credo,* and *Te Deum ;*
Chant *Miserere,* for what now so fit is
    As that or this, *Paratum est cor Meum ?*
O that thy saint would take in worth thy heart !
Thou canst not please her with a better part.
When others sing *Venite Exultemus*
    Stand by and turn to *Nolo Aemulari ;*
For *Quare fremuerunt* use *Oremus*
    Vivat Eliza for an *Ave Mary,*
And teach those swains that live about thy cell
To sing *Amen* when thou dost pray so well."

Flattery of Elizabeth is not often, except in Shakespeare, so pleasingly managed, and hardly ever so
temperate, as here ; we cannot say, as a rule, that the
courtier-poet is "happiest in fiction." Conceive that
"gracious creature," Sidney, descending to this in the
character of Therion, a forester, contending in song
with Espilus, a shepherd, for the May-Lady :

> "Two thousand deer in wildest woods I have ;
> Them can I take but you I cannot hold ;
> He is not poor who can his freedom save
> Bound but to you, no wealth but you I would,
> *But take this beast if beasts you fear to miss,*
> *For of his beasts the greatest beast he is.*
> *(Both kneeling to her Majesty.)*
> *Espilus—*
> Judge you, to whom all beauty's force is lent
> *Therion—*
> Judge you of Love to whom all love is bent."

This is not the Sidney whom we know ; the Astrophel,
the vicissitudes of whose love for Stella we can study
anew in the pretty volume, so ably edited by Mr.
Pollard. This "In Memoriam" of unavailing love is
worthy of the man of high and chivalrous courage who
wrote the letter on the French match. In Sidney's
sonnets we trace the course of a passion whose only
rival, whilst hope remains, is the patriotic fire that
longs for active service in the field. The moral might
at times be Lovelace's :

> "I could not love thee, dear, so much
> Loved I not Honour more."

Nowhere has the ennobling power of a manly and

N

worthy affection been better described than in his
words—

> " If that be sinne which doth the manners frame,
> Well staid with truth in word and faith of deed,
> Readie of wit, and fearing nought but shame ;
> If that be sinne which on fixt hearts doth breed
> A loathing of all loose unchastitie,
> Then love is sinne, and let me sinfull be."

And, when hope is gone, the struggle is never
ignoble, never undignified; the higher influences prevail, and a purer ideal at last succeeds—"*Splendidis
longum valedico nugis*," is the motto which closes the
record, when he takes farewell of earthly passion :

> ". . . let that light be thy guide
> In this small course which birth draws out to death,
> And think how evill becommeth him to slide,
> Who seeketh heav'n, and comes of heavenly breath.
> Then farewell, world ; thy uttermost I see :
> Eternall Love, maintaine thy life in me."

Sidney is the most *dramatic* of sonneteers.   In this
capacity Shakespeare and he change places.   Even
if we suppose, with Mr. Gerald Massey, that Shakespeare only occasionally writes in his own person, he
uses his art to conceal his art, to mystify rather than
to embellish, and the *result* is an effect the reverse of
dramatic.   But Sidney is constantly revealing to us
the life in which he moved, the *entourage* of that
secret passion which he bore about in the midst of
it.   He wins the prize in the tourney, in the judgment not only of his own countrymen, but of some

sent, as he says in a phrase which concentrates the very spirit of chivalry, "from that sweet enemy France." Those who are skilled in horsemanship attribute his success to this ; the townsfolk praise his strength ; jealous rivals assign all to luck; some say that his prowess is hereditary both on the father's and the mother's side; Sidney hears it all; he alone knows the reason :

> "Stella lookt on, and from her heav'nly face
> Sent forth the beames which made so faire my race."

He describes a lover's impatience in words which, with a very slight change of form, might easily pass as an excerpt from some Shakespearean scene :

> "Be your words made, good sir, of Indian ware
> That you allow me them by so small a rate ?
> Or do you cutted Spartanes imitate ?
> Or do you meane my tender eares to spare,
> That to my questions you so totall are ?
> When I demand of Phœnix Stella's state,
> You say, forsooth, you left her well of late :
> O God, thinke you that satisfies my care ?
> I would know whether she did sit or walke ;
> How cloth'd ; how waited on ; sighd she or smilde
> Whereof, with whom, how often did she talke ;
> With what pastime time's journey she beguilde ;
> If her lips daignd to sweeten my pore name.
> Say all : and all well sayd, still say the same."[1]

Sometimes he moves as a knight of the rueful

---

[1] Cf. Rosalind, in "As You Like It," iii. 2, 231 *sq.* : "What did he when thou sawest him ? What said he ? How looked he ? *Wherein went he ? Did he ask for me ?*" etc., etc.

countenance among the bright festive gatherings of
the court, and is held to be proud and reserved—

> "Because he oft in darke abstracted guise
> Seemes most alone in greatest companie."

He is teased about the current questions of the day :

> " How Ulster likes of that same golden bit
> Wherewith my father once made it halfe tame?
> If in the Scotch court be no weltring yet?
> These questions busie wits to me do frame :
> I, cumbred with good maners, answer do
> But kncw not how : for still I thinke of you."

He begs the politician who discourses to him—

> " Of courtly tides,
> Of cunning fishers in most troubled streames
> Of straying wayes, when valiant errour guides,"

to take his wisdom

> "To them that do such entertainment need."

His heart, he says—

> " —confers with Stella's beames
> And is even irkt that so sweet comedie
> By such unsuted speech should hindred be."

We had much more to say, if space permitted. We
have taken only a partial survey of these treasures.
We have wandered among the wealth which Mr.
Bullen and Mr. Pollard have shown us once more, as
a visitor to some noble mansion, who prefers the
statuary to the Dresden china.   Yet the shepherds and
shepherdesses of the Elizabethan era, though they do
plight their troth " before god Pan, and then to Church,"

are not wholly an anachronism.   The city has not yet
absorbed literature, its dust and dirt have not yet
choked up in Euterpe's flute all the stops which echo
the native sounds of the fields and woodlands.   Many
a reveller at the Mermaid could have held discourse
with Perdita amid her flowers, and knew well, when
and where to find those 'pretty daughters of the earth
and sun '—

> " The daffodils
> That come before the swallow dares, and take
> The winds of March with beauty; violets dim
> But sweeter than the lids of Juno's eyes
> Or Cytherea's breath ; pale primroses
> That die unmarried ere they can behold
> Bright Phœbus in his strength ; bold oxlips and
> The Crown Imperial."

We are still some distance from the days once so
bright and brilliant, but now like some " banquet-hall
deserted " where the candles are flickering in the
sockets, when dissolute beaux and frivolous women of
fashion monopolized the names of pastoral song.
Daphnis and Mopsus still carry with them the aroma
of the country, though sometimes, alas ! of the stable.
Nature, with her ever-fresh sources of inspiration, is
nearer to men here, even in their dreams of a life
wholly fanciful and unreal, than she condescends to
be to the brilliant epigrammatist of a later day, whose
Daphnis has gone to the town, whence no charms can
bring him back again, whose Chloe reads Rochester,
whose Phyllis has taken to paint and patches, and
whose Mopsus is a Mohawk.

A CAMBRIDGE REMINISCENCE

THIS happened in Brown's rooms at Trinity in 1865. Dalston mentioned some lines in that strange poem, Bailey's "Festus," where a certain country is compared to

> "A worm divided into parts
> That sprouts forth heads and tails but grows no hearts."

"Absurd!" cried Brown, a ' natural science" man, and prosaic—"This is the *vis formativa naturæ*, with a vengeance."

"I don't care whether it's true or not," said the more imaginative Dalston ; "I think the idea is suggestive."

"So suggestive," said Merton with a strange twinkle in his eye, "that it is the merest commonplace among the poets."

Dalston : "Indeed ? I thought I knew my poets pretty well, but I don't remember meeting with it elsewhere."

Merton : "I'll undertake to produce half-a-dozen instances out of my own reading, by this time to-morrow, if you'll come to my rooms then."

Merton was a strange creature ; very versatile and

various ; no one knew the limits of his powers or knowledge. He was a complete puzzle both to friends and examiners. He was the counterpart of Robert Browning's "Waring" in some respects, with a tinge of Shakespeare's "Puck," which made him not less mysterious, but perhaps more agreeable. He disappeared at once when he took his degree, and whether he became an Avatar in Vishnuland we have never heard.

We went to his rooms according to appointment, and he took down Milton at once from his shelves. "Now," he said, "we'll begin with Milton, and the fight in heaven with the rebel angels :

> " Cloven in twain by the Archangel's sword,
> Each half became a fiend instinct with life
> Malignant, such the vital energy
> They hold in common with the worms of earth."

He rapidly shut the volume and replaced it. " Ah!" said Dalston, "that is Milton all over—'instinct with life malignant,' though it is strange that I did not remember it." But by this time Merton had opened Wordsworth, and was reading from the "Wanderer"

> " ' See, sir,' he said,
> And pointed to the ground beneath our feet,
> ' Yon cloven worm that, writhing now in pain,
> (Unwished-for sight, yet fraught with meaning high)
> Soon, touched by Nature's healing hand, shall live
> Doubly henceforth, each half a separate whole
> Rejoicing twofold in the tempered beam
> Of this declining sun that, even now

Shining obliquely o'er the radiant earth,
(Radiant as with the fond departing smile,
Not all devoid of sadness of a friend
Who goes, nor till the morrow may return)
Seems but . . . etc.'"

WORDSWORTH, *The Wanderer*.

"Well," he broke off, "I suppose you've had enough of that?"

"I should think so," said Brown.

"I confess," said Dalston, "that I have often skipped in reading the 'Excursion.'"

"Well, but you haven't skipped, I suppose, in reading 'In Memoriam,'" answered Merton, putting Wordsworth away and beginning to read:

"If knowledge be of things we see
    Then thou and I may meet no more,
    Since Nature from an endless store
Supplies each new deficiency:

"With complex form increasing still
    And out of endless phases wrought,
    She blindly works as one self-taught
Nor cares for unity of will:

"But still to separate purpose turned
    In divers fragments of the whole,
    As myriad orbèd atoms roll
Where once a mighty Planet burned:

"In loftiest grade, in lowliest form,
    She works like one who strives for gain,
    Gleaning from ruin and from pain
In shattered globe, in severed worm.

"Yet, turning from her soulless face,
I raise my eyes as one who hears
A voice of trust beyond the years,
Re-echoed from the vast of space."

We noticed that Dalston looked very puzzled and uneasy during the reading of this passage, but Merton's rapidity of action and recitation did not allow much discussion, and he briskly took down a Byron and began :

"So he abandoned hope in earth or heaven,
And took the downward plunge, nor cursed his fate,
But with loud song and reckless laughter driven
He scoffed at bale or bliss, seeming elate
And fearless, while from every succour riven
Sheer to the depth he dropt, and Sin and Hate
Wove their dark meshes round him, yet his life
Failed not but fiercely waged redoubled strife—

  *   *   *   *   *

Like the cleft worm that dies not: (asking pardon
And trusting I may make my meaning clear
By the suggestion) fetch one from your garden,
Though it may turn, divide it without fear,
And by the morrow's sun each half will be
As neat a worm as you would wish to see."

It was Sunday evening. The chapel bell was already ringing and we should be getting on our surplices in another minute.

"Now," says Merton, 'for Shakespeare, 'Comedy of Errors' :

"'*Dromio of Ephesus.* Marry, sir ! he could *make neither head nor tail* of my reasonings, being, in respect of this, less wise than the worms that shall one day feed on him.'"

"One minute more," says Merton. "Dalston, I know, reads Dante." Shakespeare went up, and down came the Commedia.

Purgatorio :

> "Or dì Lettor, s'io non fu in forse miso,
> Questo udendo, ed il parlare oscuro,
> E siccom' al vermo ch' è per colpo diviso,
> Io guardando pur all' alto muro,
> D'un dubbio troncato due si fanno :
> Ond' io, Maestro, il senso tuo m'è duro.
> Ed egli a me. . . ."

In another moment we were scudding across the great court like the flakes of cloud severed from the main rack. "You couldn't find another anyhow," whispered Dalston to Merton as we went in.

"Wait till to-morrow," said he.

Dalston was going fishing the next day. On opening the tin box where he had put his bait, he found it all abstracted save one bisected worm.

In the lid of the box a paper, neatly inserted, contained these words in Merton's writing :

> "Puir worm thou'rt coupit clean i' twain,
> An' ilka writhin' end seems fain
> Wi' mony a warstle to complain,
>   My mair than brither,
> A head ane end maun mak' again,
>   A tail the tither !"
>   BURNS.

Moreover Merton, who had gone down that morning, left at the porter's lodge an envelope addressed to

Dalston containing, to complete the series, the following selection from Robert Browning:

" My friend, you trust too much.   Listen to this:
That hand you vow has will and power to set
Starved Ugolino and his dying sons
In breezy banquet hall at royal feast,
The outstretched hand you think has strength to draw
Laocoon from the straining serpent-folds,
The hand, I say, you follow through the world
May startle you with sudden flick i' the face
(Blue bruise for blessing on your reverent brow),
Turn key again on Ugolino's boys
With their blind father in the hungry tower,
Enwreath that other group with added coils
Fresh sprouted from the lately-severed rings
Of growth persistent,—'tis the way o' the worm.
Grub in your garden, man.   The fact will speak."

M. T.

CHISWICK PRESS:—CHARLES WHITTINGHAM AND CO.
TOOKS COURT, CHANCERY LANE, LONDON.